SETTING HIS CAP

—A—
TWIN CITIES CRYPTIDS
Novella

Aaron Rosenberg

NE❖PARADOXA
Pennsville, NJ

PUBLISHED BY
NeoParadoxa
A division of eSpec Books
PO Box 242
Pennsville, NJ 08070
www.especbooks.com

ISBN: 978-1-956463-49-1
ISBN (eBook): 978-1-956463-48-4

Copyediting: Greg Schauer, John L. French
Interior Design: Danielle McPhail
Cover Art and Design: Mike McPhail, McP Digital Graphics
Interior icon: Mike McPhail, McP Digital Graphics

Dedication

For Jenifer, Adara, and Arthur,
who put up with the creature that is me

Chapter One

Fiona McKinney grimaced as a snowball smacked her square in the face, the loose-packed missile shattering on impact to powder her in cold, wet snow. "Och, ye're a dead man!" she wailed at her boyfriend, Gary Lee, who just grinned and readied another of the frozen spheres to throw.

"You'd have to catch me first!" he shouted back, but his cry of defiance turned to a shriek as Fiona's best friend Shane Hermé tugged Gary's collar free and poured an entire handful of slushy snow down his unprotected back. "Ah, you utter pisshead!"

"Serves you right," Shane taunted, giving Fiona a big grin and a thumbs-up. "Gotcher back, Fi!" Then he screamed and ran as Gary turned on him. "Dale, sweetie, save me!"

Dale Naranji glanced up from the fire he was trying to coax to life and laughed. "Sorry, love, you're on your own against the big bad man!" He shook his head as his boyfriend fled Gary's wrath. "Hide behind Abbie, she can take him."

"Har har," Abbie Cooper replied, offering Dale a rude hand gesture in return. Yet despite that, she positioned herself to block Gary, letting Shane duck behind her powerful physique while her own boyfriend, Terry Ansalvo, lobbed snowballs at them all with mad abandon.

"Watch it, Terry!" Fiona scolded, swatting aside a lazily hurled snowball that had come wobbling her way. Brushing the last bits of Gary's attack from her cheeks and the front of her jumper, she made her way back toward their tents with as much dignity as she could manage amidst all the screaming and laughing and cursing occurring behind her. "Here you go, Dale," she said, offering him the armload of branches she'd been collecting before the impromptu combat had swept her up in its mad clutches.

"Thanks." He accepted the sticks and started feeding a few of them into the fire, which crackled greedily as it accepted this fresh tribute. "We'll need more later, for sure, but this should be enough to keep it going for now. Least long enough to cook dinner."

"Good, because I'm starved!" Fiona sank down onto a rock beside him, after first brushing it clear. Camping wasn't exactly her idea of fun — not unless it included a five-star hotel and room service! — but she was determined to make the best of it. And at least she was here with her friends. "You're really good at that," she commented, watching Dale deftly build the fire into a small but steady blaze.

"Thanks. Spent a fair bit of time out in the woods with my dad and my brother." He smiled at the memory. "The hunting part I can do without, but the camping and fishing I always liked. Something to be said for unplugging and getting back to nature."

Fiona started to say something in return, but was cut off by a strangled gasp. Glancing up, she took stock of her friends and frowned. "Where's Terry gone?" None of the others looked to be in immediate distress, which meant that odd cry must have come from him.

"Probably making more snowballs," Dale suggested. "He seems to have a shotgun approach to snowball fighting."

"I guess." Something about that sound bothered her, though, and after a second Fiona rose to her feet. "Terry?" she called out. "You okay?"

Abbie shook her head. "He's fine, Fi," she promised. "Right, babe?" But when Terry didn't answer her call, her smile slid down into a frown. "Terry?" All shenanigans forgotten, Abbie twisted around and hurried toward the edge of their little clearing, where her boyfriend had been a moment before. "Everything all right? No jokes, now, I'm serious."

Reaching the trees, Abbie shoved some branches aside, peering out into the wilderness beyond — and managed a short, desperate scream just before something yanked her off her feet and dragged her into that same undergrowth, the foliage snapping back into place as if she'd never been there.

"Abbie!" Fiona rushed forward, thinking only about helping her friend, but Gary caught her by the arm and held her back. "Let me go! Something happened to Abbie!"

"Yeah, and it'll happen to you too if you go charging after her!" Gary insisted. "Think, Fi!" He dragged her back toward the fire. "Shane, come on!"

Shane nodded and ran to their side, needing no further urging. "What the hell is going on?" he demanded, his voice shrill with burgeoning hysteria. "Is it a bear or something?"

Gary's expression was grim. "I don't know," he admitted. "But whatever it is, it got Abbie and Terry. We need to build up the fire, keep it from coming after us, too."

They had almost reached Dale and the protective blaze when something came sailing out of the woods. It slammed into Shane, hitting him hard in the small of the back and sending him stumbling forward, catching himself on his hands as he pitched toward the ground. "Ah!" he cried out, scraping his hands on the rocks and branches hidden under the snow. "What the—Oh, my God!"

Fiona didn't understand why he was screaming at first. Then she realized that the missile that had struck him was too big to be a snowball. And too dark. And glistening along one side.

It rolled to a stop, and she screamed as well, as Abbie's glazed eyes stared sightlessly up from her severed head.

Fiona was still screaming as several short, stocky figures slid from the woods and stomped toward them, their footsteps echoing loudly. They all had long hair in various shades of blonde and red, and wore sturdy clothes of leather and wool—and each of them had a dark red hat perched atop their head.

But two had hats that looked oddly wet, as if they had been sprayed with water. Only far, far darker.

That sight triggered memories of old stories for Fiona. Stories her grandmother had told her, dark and filled with violence and pain. Stories of strange little men with big iron boots and blood-red caps— and an appetite for murder.

"Wh-what do you want?" Gary managed to bluster, putting himself in front of Fiona and pushing her back toward where Dale waited. Shane had staggered to his feet, and she grabbed his hand, tugging him back with her. She tried to think what they could use to fend off what looked like a small gang of feral, bloodthirsty kids. Maybe they could light something, make a torch?

One of the kids darted forward, then. They leapt into the air, higher than should have been possible—and came down with a crashing kick to her boyfriend's head. Fiona heard an awful, heartrending crunch, and Gary toppled to the ground, his skull clearly caved in by the fearsome blow.

She screamed again.

Then the strangers were on her, and Shane and Dale as well. The fire didn't help. Her fingernails did nothing but make them laugh. Fiona died in a flurry of blows, her broken body joining her friends' there on the blood-strewn snow of the campsite.

"Och, that were too easy!" Brodie Adair grumbled, but he did so with a grin, hunkering down over Fiona's cooling body. Tugging off his cap, he swabbed it in her blood before setting the now-drenched item back atop his head.

"Still fun," his twin sister Lilas countered, wetting her cap in Shane's blood just an arm's length away. "An' what else were we ta do, what with them being so accommodating about it all?"

"Aye, they all but bared their throats to us, the wee bairns," their uncle Finlay agreed, soaking his own cap on Gary's shattered brow. "Fools, ta camp in our woods withou' our permission."

Finlay's son Logan snorted. "As if we'd grant such!" He'd been the first to wet his cap, when Terry had carelessly stepped out of the others' sight to sweep up an armful of snow. The young lad had barely even registered the Red Caps' presence before an iron boot had cracked his skull and snapped his neck in the process.

"All good?" Aunt Blaire asked, and the others nodded. "Right, then let's clean this up an' head back home."

"What about...?" Brodie's younger sister Elidh asked, and flinched at her aunt's glare but did not back down. "We should bring ought back for him, aye?"

The others scowled and shook their heads, but no one stopped Elidh as she found a canteen among the camping gear, emptied it of the tepid water within, and used it to scoop up some of Dale's blood. Then she carefully set the gory vessel aside to help dispose of the bodies and any trace of the violence she and her kin had just committed upon the hapless campers. They also gathered anything they thought might be useful, to bring with them.

"Ye spoil him, ye know," Brodie warned after they'd finished, the site completely clear once more, and Elidh had collected the canteen.

She nodded but kept a tight grip on it anyway. What else could she do? Someone had to be looking out, and no one else was willing, so it fell to her.

With a sigh, Elidh followed the others as they began the short trek back.

CHAPTER TWO

THE TWINS BICKERED GOOD-NATUREDLY MOST OF THE WAY HOME, AS THEY often did, but just below the crest of the final hill Finlay held up a hand and all conversation ceased. He nodded to Logan, who crept forward until only the tip of his nose and the peak of his cap edged over the rise. He lay still a moment or two before nodding and popping to his feet.

"All clear!" he declared, the second word still emerging from his mouth as he suddenly darted over and down the hill, laughing as he went. "Race ya!" came trailing back behind him along the heather.

"Och, ye stinker!" Brodie and Lilas were after him in a flash, and Elidh joined them, shouting for sheer joy as her legs pumped and ate up the distance to their home, nestled into the hills along the bank below. Castle Lachlan was a fine old place, and their family had claimed it after the Battle of Culloden, when shells had torn it to pieces. But it was still picturesque—and still technically the MacLachlans' principal home, even though that human clan had built a new castle a few years later, just over the next rise—so they had to be wary of tourists and any others.

Now, with no one around, the Adairs could openly approach, whooping and hollering the whole way.

As Logan neared the thick stone walls there came a deep, grating sound, and the massive iron gates parted. He zoomed for the narrow gap there, passing through it only a few body lengths ahead of his cousins. "The winner!" he shouted, spinning about and nearly toppling from his own momentum.

"You cheated!" Lilas argued, not-so-accidentally crashing into him. Brodie piled on top, and it was all Elidh could do not to trip and join the heap of her kin.

Finlay and Blaire brought up the rear, and Great-Uncle Karson shoved the gates closed again behind them. "Good hunt?" he asked, limping over to join them, his right boot scraping on the cobblestones and sending up a small shower of sparks. He'd been mauled by a werewolf when small, and his leg had never healed quite right.

"Aye," Finlay replied with a laugh, tugging his cap free and tossing it into a high spin. Catching the headgear, he reached inside and drew out a fistful of gleaming golden coins that hadn't been there before his kill. "See?"

"Well done." Karson couldn't quite hide the envy in his gaze or his voice, but he patted his nephew on the shoulder anyway. "Come deposit it all, then."

The older Red Cap turned away, leading them across the courtyard to what had once been a lesser hall—and was now the treasury. The heavy oak door had long since been repaired, complete with a stout lock, and he used a thick key to open that, tugging the door back to reveal the mounds upon mounds of gold and silver heaped carelessly within.

Nothing loath, Finlay stepped up and tossed his handful of treasure in among the rest. He dug in his cap again and came up with more, which followed the first batch. A third try yielded only a single coin, but it still gleamed and shone as he flung it into the room.

Blaire was next, and her haul was much the same, as each of them had claimed one victim's blood for their caps. Then Logan, Brodie, Lilas, and finally Elidh, since they traditionally went in age order.

After their caps were empty, they deposited the scavenged food and camping gear in the storeroom across the way. Then, patting the canteen she'd retained, Elidh glanced toward the ruined old tower at the castle's center.

Karson caught her look. "Aye, he's up there, the pathetic sod." He spat to the side. "If ye must see him, go on with ye."

That was as close to permission as she was likely to get, so Elidh wasted no time hurrying toward the tower's small, arched door. Slipping through the entrance, she closed it carefully behind her—not that any of the others were likely to waste their time following.

Then she began to climb.

The tower's roof had long since crumbled away, as had parts of two walls, but the single upper floor was still solid, and bits of the side still crept up and offered some shade. From here one could see the entire end of Loch Fyne spread out before them, and on a clear day even make out the Isle of Jura away to the west, or the Isle of Arran equally far to the south. Glasgow was a series of blocks and spires in the east, smoke billowing from the many factories and plants there. That was as close as any of the Adairs wished to come to such a hive of humanity.

But right now, Elidh's focus was entirely upon the small, slight figure perched at the tower's edge and huddled within a thick wool coat, legs dangling over the side, iron boots scraping the walls with each feeble kick.

"Hullo, Knox," she called softly, so as not to startle him. He glanced back over his shoulder, and a weak smile crossed his lips.

"Heya, Elidh," her baby brother replied. "All okay, then?"

"All good." She approached carefully, cautiously, the way one might a wild animal—or a wounded one. Stopping right behind him, she rested a hand on his shoulder, and proffered the canteen with her other. "Brought ye somat."

She was close enough to see his grimace. "I dinna want it, but thankee."

"Take it." She scowled down at him, at his pallor, at the way his hands shook. "Ye'll die without it!"

He shrugged. "So, I'll die. At least I'll not 'ave bought my life with that of others."

That was quite enough of that. Baring her teeth, Elidh snatched Knox's cap right off his head. "Hey!" he protested, but was too slow and too weak to stop her or to take it back as she stomped back toward the small room's center. There she popped the canteen's lid and up-ended it over her brother's hat. Her collection had been rushed and sloppy, and the choice of container hardly ideal, but even so a cupful dribbled from the canteen's mouth to slick the cap's surface. Once she was sure it was empty, Elidh tossed the vessel aside, rubbing the hat's sides together to distribute the blood as evenly as possible, though she was careful not to press too hard and dry it all out. Then she shoved it back on her little brother's head.

"There!" Her task done, she dropped to the floor beside him and wrapped an arm around his narrow shoulders. "Feel better?"

She could tell he didn't want to admit it, but he took a breath—and kept breathing in, straightening as he did. His color improved, and his hands steadied. "Yes," he answered finally, his voice soft as a whisper but far stronger than it had been. "Thank you." He tilted his head enough to tap his temple to hers, their matching red-blonde hair mingling.

"Of course." She waited a moment before shifting away, lowering her arm so she could turn and face him better. "Now, show me what ye've been working on."

That brought a brighter smile, as Knox lifted the large drawing pad — a treasure he'd smuggled out of the storeroom many years ago — from his other side. "Here," he said, flipping it open and turning pages until he reached an image of a small black dog with floppy ears and bright eyes.

"Oh! Snapper!" They'd found the pup when a camper had brought him along into the woods and had rescued him from their family's intent to either kill him or just abandon him. Elidh and Knox had brought him home instead, feeding him on scraps, playing with him, taking turns sleeping with him cuddled to their chests. They had loved the little dog fiercely.

He had survived almost a full year before a cousin crushed the pup beneath his boot, though whether out of malice or mere carelessness they'd never know.

Now, looking at the image, Elidh almost expected to see Snapper wag his little brush tail and yip his sharp little bark. "It's perfect," she said, brushing at her eyes. "Like he's come back to life."

Knox smiled and carefully tore the page free, handing it to her. "Here. He's yours."

"Oh." It had been a long time since anyone had given her anything that wasn't purely practical, and Elidh clasped the picture to her chest. "Thank you."

A deep, rich sound pealed up from below, the ringing of a heavy iron bell by an equally heavy boot. "Come on," she said, scrambling to her feet and tugging her brother to his. "Best eat afore it's all gone."

Knox grimaced. "If I must." He was clearly not eager to descend into the familial chaos that awaited, and Elidh could not entirely blame him. But he still needed to eat. They both did. So she ignored his half-hearted protest and dragged him to the stairs.

But she was careful to detour to her bed first, once they were down, to hide the sketch beneath her pillow.

CHAPTER THREE

KNOX STEELED HIMSELF AS BEST HE COULD BEFORE FOLLOWING HIS SISTER into the great hall.

It didn't help.

"Oy, there's the wee wanker!" That was Brodie, always the first to give him grief, and the loudest. Hard to believe he'd once paraded Knox around on his shoulders and sung him to sleep. "Where've ye been hiding, eh? Among the taters and neeps?" One of the aforementioned tubers came hurtling across the room, slamming Knox in the shoulder with enough force to bruise but not quite enough to knock him back a step. That was something, anyway.

"Aye, been weeping and wailing and tearing at yer pretty hair?" Lilas joined in. After all, anything her twin did, she had to do better. Including torment Knox. "Yer like a wee girl, aintcha? No' much good fer anything." The fact that she was female herself clearly had no bearing on the insult.

Knox ignored them as best he could, trailing after Elidh to the side table, where he accepted the bowl and cup rudely shoved his way by one of his aunts. Not Blaire, she'd have brained him with the heavy dishes instead. Nor did the fact that he'd slaved away helping prepare the meal lessen the server's scorn. Such chores were normally only for the very young or the infirm, and Knox was neither, even if most of the time his cap was subject to just enough sprinkled blood to keep him barely alive.

The clan was all gathered at long trestle tables before the raised platform where Ailie, Knox's great-grandmother and the clan's Matriarch, ate alone. He and Elidh managed to squeeze onto the back end of the farthest one, closest to the room's outer wall. A sharp wind blew in through the wide window arches there, biting as a hungry wolf, but the light of the torches and candelabras barely reached and Knox hoped he'd be able to hide in the shadows and eat in peace.

Unsurprisingly, he was not that lucky.

He'd managed only a few spoonfuls of the stew — the meat today was duck, which he knew because he'd been the one tasked with plucking and dressing it — when someone slapped the back of his head, sending him crashing into the table. His spoon went flying and soup sloshed from the bowl onto his lap.

"Food's for clan only," Logan's voice drifted over his shoulder. "That means Red Caps. And ye ain't one."

Knowing there was no good response, no safe answer, Knox opted for bravado, hoping that would at least earn him points with some of the others. "I've got a cap, same as you." Pushing the bowl safely away, he turned to face his attacker. "Got boots, too — same as you." And he lashed out with the left, the iron toe slamming into Logan's knee.

"Ah, ye little turd!" A hand grabbed for him, but pain had his cousin off balance and Knox easily ducked aside. He twisted off the bench, hopping back and away as Logan shook his head and straightened, murder in his eyes. "I'll wear *yer* blood on my cap!" he roared, stomping forward.

Only to find another Red Cap blocking his path. One far older and stronger than Logan himself. Old enough to have facial hair, which was rare among their kind.

"Nae, ye'll no' lay a hand on yer kin," Fraser Adair declared, thick arms crossed over his broad chest. Though his thick red hair and equally dense beard were shot through with white, age had only toughened him, like a weathered tree trunk. "Sit ye down. Now."

Logan grumbled but didn't dare argue. Instead, with a single glare at Knox, he backed away, toward his own vacated seat.

Knox waited until his cousin had gone before turning to his savior. "Thanks, Da."

But Fraser waved off the statement. "I didna do it for ye," he stated, not even glancing in Knox's direction. "But ta save the clan from strife." He stomped away without another word.

And that was the most civil — and the most words — Knox had had from his father in years.

With a sigh, Knox returned to his seat and his meal. He had no appetite, but knew he had to eat. The cap could only do so much on its own.

The hush that had fallen over the room during the brief conflict began to fade away, conversations starting back up here and there. By the time Knox had finished his stew, using the hard, dark roll he'd been given atop it to sop up the last bits, everything seemed back to normal, and he started to let himself relax a little. Some nights were better than others, and this was looking to be one of those.

He should have known better.

"Knox Adair!" His name rang out, startling him and everyone else, the silence dropping over them all like a thick blanket, smothering any other noise. "Approach me!"

There was no mistaking that voice, or the tone of command it carried, and so, despite wishing to be anywhere else, Knox rose to his feet and slowly made his plodding way down the hall and up to the very front.

To the throne of the Matriarch.

Ailie peered down at him. She was ancient, well over three centuries, yet still hale enough to lead hunts and bring down prey unassisted. Her cap hung down almost to her shoulders, its sides permanently stretched out after years of treasure bulging up from within. Her long braids were snow-white, but her glacial blue eyes were sharp. At her side, Logan and Brodie lurked, sporting matching grins that twisted Knox's innards just to see. What were the two of them up to now?

"Come here," Ailie ordered, and Knox hopped up onto the dais. She reached out a gnarled, but steady hand and caught his chin between pincer-like fingers, tugging him closer until their foreheads nearly touched. Her gaze bored into him.

"Och, ye're pale as a ghost, and thin as a twig! When was the last time ye hunted?" his great-grandmother demanded, still holding him fast, and Knox shuddered. He remembered the last time all too well.

So, apparently, did others. "It was ten years ago, Matriarch," Logan supplied. "His crucible."

"Crucible." What an awful, evil use of the word. Every Red Cap was made to hunt upon their twelfth birthday. They wore their boots and cap for the first time that day and could not return until they had killed something and bathed both items in its blood. That was what bonded the boots to them and what gave the caps their power. The Red Cap could not pick what to hunt, it had to be the first suitable creature to cross their path. For some, that was a rabbit. For others, a deer. For those who were very, very lucky, a human.

Young Knox, clumsy in his heavy iron boots with his dry, clean cap hanging over his eyes, had stumbled upon a beaver.

The poor creature had stared at him as he'd approached, its small eyes calm and wise. Knox had seen beavers before. They were gentle creatures, though protective of their young, and careful, even cautious. Not a threat to anyone at all.

He would have turned away, found something else. But his father and siblings were all crowded nearby, far enough back to give him space but close enough to watch. They would never have let him leave it unharmed.

It had taken two kicks with his new boots to kill the beaver. Knox's head had been swimming and his stomach heaving the entire time. He'd barely finished dipping his cap and sliding his boots through the blood before he'd been violently sick.

He spent the next three days shivering and miserable, throwing up anything and everything. He nearly died.

Sometimes, in his darkest moments, Knox wished he had.

He had never hunted again.

"Tha' is no' right," his great-grandmother declared now, shaking his head. His jaw hurt from the pressure of her fingers. "Ye are a Red Cap of Clan Adair. Ye must hunt, and ye must kill." Finally, she released him, and Knox stumbled back a step, rubbing at his aching chin. "In two days, ye'll lead the hunt," Ailie announced to all those assembled, which was the entire family. "Ye'll kill, and ye'll properly soak yer cap." Her gaze flicked up to his hat, which even after Elidh's help was only mildly damp.

"He cannae do it," Logan muttered. "He dinna have the stones."

There was nothing wrong with the Matriarch's ears. "If he dinna," she stated now, "he'll be banished fore'er, an Adair nae more."

With that settled, she turned away, dismissing Knox from her sight and her thoughts all at once. Others began filtering out of the hall, Logan and Brodie and Lilas giving him nasty smirks as they went. Soon only Knox and Elidh were left as Knox abandoned all decorum to drop down onto his rump there on the lip of the dais.

He looked over at his sister, the only family who even cared. "Oh, Elidh," he wailed as she approached. "What'm I gonna do?"

CHAPTER FOUR

ELIDH PUT AN ARM AROUND HIM BUT DIDN'T REPLY. WHAT WAS THERE TO say, really?

"Would it be so verah bad, then?" she asked finally, her voice soft. "Ta go through with it? Just this once? They'd all leave ye alone after that, ye know. Brodie and Logan and Lilas. They'd have naught more ta say, not once Great-Grandma declared ye fit and good."

Knox only buried his face in his hands. "I know," he agreed, his voice muffled through his fingers. "You're right. It would solve everything. But I can't, Elidh. I just can't!" He glanced up, his face streaked with tears—just in time to catch a blow across the cheek that sent him reeling to the floor.

When he was able to blink away the tears and blood and hair, Knox saw his father standing over him, face purpling with rage, chest heaving with anger.

"How dare ye?" the older Adair snarled down at him, fists clenched and ready to strike again. "Sitting here, sniveling like some wee human bairn, whinging about how hard yer life is? As if ye had any right to tha' life in the first place!"

"Da—" Elidh started, half-rising, but their father held up a hand and she subsided, unable to push past his paternal authority.

"Yer a Red Cap, and an Adair, by the sun and the stars," he stated instead, leaning in close so his face was inches from Knox's own, and the fury in his eyes burned the air between them. "Grow a pair and act like it, fer once. Ye owe her tha' much, at least."

With that last dagger hurled, he straightened and stormed off, his boots echoing on the stone floor. Knox didn't budge for a long while, just staring after him. Eventually, Elidh overcame her own paralysis and helped him sit up. "It wasn't your fault," she reminded him, as she had many times over the years. Not that Fraser would ever believe that.

In his mind, his youngest child had murdered his wife whilst being born, and that was all there was to it.

Nor, Knox realized as he slowly stood and brushed away the blood from his torn cheek—already healing, thanks to what Elidh had brought him earlier—would going on the hunt help in that regard. Even if the rest of the clan accepted him, his own father never would. Nor would a single killing erase the years of abuse he'd endured from his other kin, or their own views on him. Sooner or later, they'd start in again, and it would grow worse and worse until Ailie made another such proclamation.

He couldn't bear such a nasty, bloody cycle.

"I cannae stay," he said softly, and once the words were out, he knew them to be true. "Elidh, I cannae stay." He took both her hands in his own. "I'm sorry. It's best for everyone if I go."

"Go?" she stared, so much like him in eye and jaw and hair. Yet, though she could be tender, even sweet, she had never once agonized over the killing the way he did. This life suited her. "Go where? How? Knox, ye'll die!"

He knew what she meant, of course. Without her bringing him blood, he'd weaken and sicken even more, until finally his cap dried out completely. The second that happened, his heart would simply stop.

There were, he decided, worse ways to go.

"I'll figure somat out," he promised her, clutching her hands tighter before releasing them and stepping back. "I'm no' lookin' ta die, Elidh. But this, stayin' here—it's already killing me. Just slower." He offered her a quick, shy smile. "Ye're the only thing I'll regret leaving."

And, he didn't add, her own life would improve when she no longer had to protect him from the others. She'd be free as well.

"Tha' dinna answer me other questions," she pointed out, her face set in a scowl, but Knox knew that look. It meant his sister had accepted something she didn't like but couldn't find a way around. She wouldn't try to stop him. "Where'll ye go? An' how'll ye survive?" *Without me to kill for you,* hung in the air unsaid.

"I dinna know," he conceded. "But I'll think a' something." Hurrying from the hall with her beside him, Knox headed to his own bed—tucked away in the little alcove behind Elidh's, so she could wake and stop the others tormenting him during the night. How many years had she been forced to play surrogate mother because their own was dead and gone — his fault, at least in part — and he was too weak to defend himself?

No more.

Knox had very little, both because the clan believed in communal rather than personal wealth and because as the runt and the reject he always came last. Tugging up the bedsheet, he tucked his precious pad into it, along with the handful of pencils and chalks he and Elidh had scrounged over the years, and tied that around his body to keep the bundle safe and secure against his back. When he turned away, his sister had her cap off and was rummaging within it.

"What're ye — Don't," he warned, glancing about them in case anyone else saw. "If anyone finds out…"

"They won't," she promised, and came up at last with a single gold coin. "Here. For food and such like." And she pressed it into his palm.

Knox nodded, closing his fingers around the gift. Then he hugged her quickly and slid past, heading not for the heavy front gate but for the ruin's rear. The walls there had crumbled away, leaving only a handful of stone blocks in places, easy enough for even him to step over.

At the sleeping chamber's door, he looked back, knowing she would still be watching. "Take care of yerself, Elidh," he told her, which was as close as an Adair could come to expressing love.

"And ye, Knox," she replied, her eyes as wet as he knew his to be. "I'll think on ye."

He nodded, then ducked away before either of them could say or do anything foolish — and before anyone else could stumble upon the strange scene and wonder what it meant.

Moments later, Knox had clambered through a gap in the outer wall and was hiking down the hill and away from the only home he'd ever known. He had no idea what the future held, but just knowing that gloomy old castle, with its legacy of blood and death and violence, was forever behind him felt like a great weight off his shoulders. There was a spring in his step as he clumped downhill, his iron boots kicking up clods of dirt and grass, and the air felt clean and clear like after a rainstorm.

It felt like a new beginning.

CHAPTER FIVE

TWO DAYS LATER, KNOX ADMITTED THAT HIS NEW BEGINNING MIGHT HAVE got off to a rocky start.

He'd only been outside the castle on short forays since his disastrous "crucible," which meant he had no familiarity anymore with rough terrain, wilderness, hiking, or any of it, really. And though Elidh's gift had certainly kept him alive, it hadn't been enough to truly soak his cap — not that he'd wanted it to! — so his strength and stamina were still pitiful for a Red Cap.

It was also the end of winter, and still freezing out, though just warm enough for any remaining snow and ice to turn into slush. And all he had was his wool coat to protect him from the elements.

Despite that, he'd managed to march his way up the rest of Loch Fyne, past Inveraray to Cairndow. Initially, he'd considered going south instead and striking out toward Glasgow. The idea of finally seeing the city had intrigued him, but he'd realized it would be a terrible idea. He knew nothing about cities, or people in general. Surviving had to come first, and that would be simpler someplace smaller, more rural, where he'd have an easier time observing and figuring out how to adapt. He could visit Glasgow later, if he wanted.

So, instead, Knox had gone north, but only to the loch's edge. From there he'd turned east, cutting across Scotland.

He'd been lucky in that there weren't that many settlements out this way. It was still largely farmland, or mountains. He'd spied a few small villages but had chosen to steer clear of them for now.

A rainstorm caused a new complication, bringing slightly warmer temperatures but washing the blood from his cap. Knox knew that meant trouble, but he still couldn't bring himself to kill something just so he could live a little longer.

Instead, with flagging strength, he tromped through woods and grass, searching for a lucky break.

He found one when he stumbled upon a badger feasting on a large rabbit. The vicious animal snarled at Knox, baring its impressive teeth and raising one clawed paw, but after years of enduring his kin, Knox was hardly afraid of such things.

"Get out of here!" he yelled, stomping hard on the ground. A rock cracked under his iron sole and the sound echoed like a gunshot, startling the badger. It reared up, then turned tail and fled into the safety of the woods.

Knox wasted no time crouching by the dead rabbit. "I'm sorry," he whispered as he pulled off his cap and dipped it in the wreck of the body's midsection, where fresh blood still pooled. "Thank you." Restoring the grisly hat to his head, he straightened, feeling the rush of renewed strength that always came with such an awful act. He'd worried that he wouldn't be able to stomach even that much, but it seemed the fact that he hadn't harmed the poor animal himself was enough for him to overcome his queasiness.

Now, at least, he could go on.

The next day went much the same. Knox hiked as long and as far as he could before finding a sturdy tree and climbing up among its branches to sleep. It was cold, but walking kept him just warm enough, and at night he huddled within his coat. He ate whatever mushrooms and berries and nuts he could find as he walked, and drank from ponds and streams whenever he chanced across them.

Twice he encountered dead animals, one killed by an apparent fall and the other by predators, and paused to dip his cap, murmuring thanks each time. The first of those was a bit rough, a fledgling pigeon he had to carve open with a sharp rock, but Knox told himself it was no worse than dressing a dead bird or gutting a fish. His stomach still roiled, but he managed.

Then he came across a campsite. It had two tents set up, their cheerful nylon sides almost glowing against the greenery all around. A fire had been laid but not yet lit, as it was mid-day. No one was about, and Knox took advantage of the moment to sneak into the nearer tent and rummage through the two backpacks there. They both contained clothes, as he'd hoped, but far too large for him.

The two bags in the second tent were smaller and festooned with cartoonish images, however, and Knox guessed they belonged to children. He dug in one and pulled out a pair of jeans, a T-shirt with another cartoon image on it, and a red flannel shirt. They looked close enough to his own size, so he took them — but not before fishing around in his cap and extracting Elidh's gold coin, which he left in their place.

The next day, having bathed in a stream, brushed his ragged coat as best he could, and dressed in his newly acquired clothes, Knox risked entering a town for the first time.

"Och, should ye no' be in school, lad?" was the first thing a person outside his own family ever said to him, the words called out by an old man working outside in front of a small, neat stone house. Knox wasn't really sure how to reply to that, so he just waved and kept walking.

There were more houses, and actual roads — something he'd never seen up close before, the treated and sealed ground flat and hard beneath his boots — and here and there he saw other people, too, out walking or even driving. Knox had heard of cars from some of the others, but he'd never seen one, and nearly froze at the first sight of the boxy metal vehicle as it whisked past on its big, round wheels, belching a cloud of foul black smoke behind it. How did people stand such things?

Not sure where to go or what to do, he simply continued on. All of the dwellings were one or two stories tall and made of stone, brick, or both. There were shops, too — also something he'd heard of but never seen — and most of those had larger windows and signs above the door proclaiming their purpose.

When he saw one that said only "Fresh fish," Knox had a sudden idea. One he wondered why he'd never thought of before.

Entering the little shop, he found it clean and tidy, with white-washed walls, swept tile floors, and glass cases at the front showing fish on beds of ice. It smelled heavily of fish, of course, but that was to be expected. A stout woman stood behind the case by the back, next to a heavy register, and frowned when he entered, despite the cheerful tinkling of a bell on the door.

"This is no' a sweets shop, lad," she told him, though her tone didn't seem mean, just brisk. "Best run along."

Knox approached instead, and saw her eyes widen as he got close enough for her to make out his features clearly. "I was wondering if ye might need help with anythin'," he asked, taking his cap off and holding it in both hands. "I'm a hard worker, and I don't mind getting dirty."

"And how old are ye, exactly?" she asked, leaning on the counter to study him.

He had to think about that one, since birthdays were rarely marked among his clan after that all-important twelfth one. "Twenty-two," he answered finally.

She laughed. "And ye've got ID to prove it, have ye?" She saw the answer on his face—was that even a thing?—and shook her head. "Unless ye've got somat to prove it, I cannae hire ye, lad. E'en though I could use the help, in truth."

"Ah." Knox stuck the cap back on his head. "I understand." He didn't, really, but suspected there wasn't much to be done about that.

He was just turning back toward the door when she spoke again. "Unless ye'd be willing to work for cash?"

Cash? Oh, paper money—others had brought such back a time or two, after a hunt, though it had been quickly discarded with any other rubbish. The clan only cared for the gold they pulled from their caps. But humans, they dealt in such things, and he caught the inference—cash versus whatever official process she couldn't use for him. "Aye, cash'd be fine."

"Well, then." She studied him again, though this time with a more critical eye. "How are ye at cleanin' fish?"

As that was exactly the job he'd hoped for, Knox smiled. "Good. I'm good at it." Which wasn't a lie—fish from the loch had been the clan's primary source of protein and Knox had often been relegated to the worst aspects of kitchen duty, including cleaning and prepping their catches.

"Right." She lifted a section of the counter and beckoned him back behind the display. "Come on, then, and we'll see. I'm Linda." She held out her hand, and Knox shook it once he'd joined her.

"Knox. Nice ta meetcha." Then he followed her back through a door into the rear of the shop, where freshly caught fish lay waiting to be cleaned and filleted. He'd never had any qualms about fishing—they'd never struck him as feeling creatures the way rabbits and foxes did — so he didn't hesitate when Linda handed him a slim-bladed knife and waved him toward a large, handsome perch. It was messy work, which he'd not only expected but counted on.

After all, fish had blood, too.

CHAPTER SIX

MARCH 2017

TWO WEEKS LATER, KNOX SAT AT A SMALL TABLE OUTSIDE A LITTLE SHOP, enjoying the sunshine high overhead, the crisp air, and the chance to take a break.

Linda had proven to be a taskmaster, taking full advantage of her new employee's unofficial status to heap all the worst jobs upon him. Which was not to say she was any worse than Great-Uncle Karson or Great-Aunt Greer, who had been in charge of most daily tasks at the castle. Linda, at least, was not mean about it, or vicious. She had nothing against Knox. There was simply a lot to do around the shop, and since she was paying him, she figured she might as well get the most out of his efforts.

He didn't mind. They were all things he'd done before, and for far less appreciation—and no pay beyond the dubious honor of being allowed to live with his kin. And, as he'd hoped but would never have dared try back at the castle even if it'd occurred to him, fish blood proved a decent substitute for animal or human—he was able to soak his cap each day without any trouble, and felt stronger than he had in ages, though probably still weaker than any other Red Cap would. The work was exhausting, that was all. Most nights, Knox was so beat he had to drag himself upstairs to the small room Linda had given him, where he immediately collapsed on the bed, sleeping straight through until the old alarm clock on the little table there roused him in the morning.

Plus, there were so many new things to learn! Having grown up in it, Knox had never realized just how primitive his life had been. Bathing had occurred when it rained, when you fell in the loch, or when someone said you stank, and if not in the loch it involved sluicing yourself with buckets of ice-cold water. Clothes had been cast-offs from the victims of their hunts, cut down to suit their smaller size. Entertainment consisted of foraging, hunting, fishing, running around, and playing simple games like cards or dice. He only knew how to read because some of the elders considered it necessary for identifying items taken from their kills.

The first night here, alone in his little room, it had taken Knox a good twenty minutes to figure out how the toilet worked. Mastering the shower had been quicker but more alarming, since he'd been standing fully clothed in the tub when he'd succeeded in turning the water on.

If Linda had noticed his bedraggled state when he'd first arrived, she hadn't said anything. But after watching her and her customers, Knox began to adjust his appearance and behavior to match them more closely. Showers every morning — the hot water was a revelation! — and hair combed out and tied back out of his face, hands scrubbed, clothes as neat as he could get them.

There was a small shop down the road that sold clothes and basic items, but even better was the Oxfam Linda had pointed him toward after handing over his first week's pay. Everything there was used but clean, far less expensive than new, and they had no problem accepting cash — which Knox had been forced to wait for, since even though the fish blood proved enough to sustain him, it apparently wasn't potent enough to generate any sort of coinage. He didn't like paper currency much but having it in his pocket once Linda had paid him had still felt better than not having any. Not that a lot of people carried cash, apparently.

That had been another big discovery. Credit cards. The first time he'd seen a customer hand Linda one, Knox had no idea what it meant. He'd watched her run it, however, and understood that it was money of some sort. But how? And how did one get one? He hadn't dared ask her, for fear of exposing his ignorance and inviting questions about his upbringing, but he'd paid attention whenever he was out in the front room or could peek out the door from the back and had seen that people could use either that or bills and coins to pay.

Then, one time, someone Linda hadn't known had used one, and she'd asked to see ID along with it. That was what she'd mentioned when he'd shown up, but he hadn't seen or heard of one since, so Knox was particularly interested as the man handed over a second card, one with his picture on it. Linda had glanced at it, compared it to the credit card, then processed the payment and returned both along with his purchase. Knox had more questions than ever after that. Did everyone have ID, or just people from out of town? Why didn't she ask to see anyone else's? What else was the ID for? And how did you get one?

Midway through his first week, he'd been sweeping in back when Linda had poked her head in. "I'mma run to the grocer's for a sec," she'd said. "Mind the front. You know how?"

"On it," he'd replied, and had set the broom aside to go perch on the stool behind the front counter, by the register. No one had come in before she'd returned, which was probably for the best, but two days later she'd called him up again, this time when she was there and dealing with an older woman he'd seen before.

"Ring up the sale," Linda had instructed, and Knox had obeyed, copying what he'd seen her do and punching keys on the register to tally the amount and then the woman's pay and her change. It had dinged and popped open its cash drawer, and he'd taken the woman's money—a twenty-pound note—and counted out her change in bills and coins, handing those over with the receipt.

"Good," Linda had said once the woman had gone. "Next chance I've got a card, I'll have you do it to make sure you've got that down, too." As that meant both an additional skill and a chance to examine one of the cards up close, Knox was happy to comply.

Technology was another major adjustment. Linda had the radio going throughout the day, playing music. Knox had been mystified that first morning, wondering where the musicians were hiding. He did know music—various kin played fiddle, banjo, guitar, pipes, or drums, and sometimes there were impromptu performances on a pleasant evening—but he'd never heard it in such variety, or so polished, and the whole concept of it emanating from a little box was baffling. Clearly, it was some kind of magic. The register was just a mechanical device, that much Knox understood, and so was the little credit card machine, but the first time Linda answered her phone he froze in fear. What devilry was this? He'd seen it enough times since to gather that it was a device, too, and let her communicate with people far away. He just wasn't sure how.

On his first day off, end of that first week, Knox had spent the morning sleeping and the afternoon roaming the town, acquiring things like clothes and toiletries—Linda had provided a small list without a word, a clear hint that whatever a toothbrush was, he should invest in one—and trying to make sense of his new surroundings, at least enough so he wouldn't gawk every time he exited the shop.

The town was called Kinglassie. To hear Linda's customers talk, it was a small place and fairly limited, with only a few thousand residents, a single school, and a handful of shops.

Knox had never even imagined so many could live in such a small area together. He was constantly amazed at just how many people were around. And the cars! The shop was right on the main road—called "Main Street," conveniently enough—and the vehicles went back and forth throughout the day, rumbling and belching and rattling so loudly he could barely hear himself think.

That was why today, as he'd roamed with no clear intent, he'd been pleased to spot this place on a side street instead. It was a plain, one-story building with clean, whitewashed walls and a wide brick courtyard. The shop had large windows along the front and tables and chairs set up inside, but on a day like this Knox liked the idea of sitting outside instead.

He'd learned how to use the strange paper money by now, and had barely faltered at going inside, up to the counter there, and ordering a coffee and a cinnamon bun. The girl behind the counter had smiled at him, and a minute later he was taking his purchases and seating himself at one of the round metal tables on the patio.

Coffee was something he'd only discovered since working for Linda. "Cannae manage without my morning cuppa," she'd told him that first day after brewing a pot and offering him a mug. Knox knew tea, of course, and water, and ale, but one taste of the strong, sharp, dark brew and he was hooked.

Now, taking a sip, he sighed. This wasn't so bad a life, really. He had a place to stay, work, money for food, a way to keep his cap wet. He missed Elidh, of course, but not having to constantly worry about attacks from his cousins and other siblings was a blessing.

Not having to face his father's disapproval every day even more so.

And now, with time to spare, Knox did something else he hadn't done since leaving the castle. He took out his sketchpad, flipped it open to the next blank page, selected one of his pencils, and began to draw. A few quick lines and the fish shop's interior swam into view. Linda was there behind the counter, haggling with a customer whose back was to the viewer, a fillet already set out on paper and ready to be wrapped up and taken away.

Knox was so intent upon his art that he didn't realize the café girl had approached until he heard her gasp. Glancing up, he saw she'd come up behind him, coffeepot in hand, but she was staring at the drawing instead.

"Tha's amazin'!" she told him breathlessly, her eyes wide. "It's like I'm there!"

"Thanks." Elidh was the only person who'd ever appreciated his art before, and Knox flushed at the attention.

"Can ye do others?" the girl asked now, taking the chair alongside without asking. Though it *was* her café, after all. She was younger than him, Knox guessed, though not by much, and had dark eyes, dark brows, but hair almost as blonde as his own. "Like, could ye do a dragon or somat?"

"A dragon?" Knox laughed. "Well, I've never seen one of those, have I? But aye, no reason not." Turning to the next page, he began to sketch out a long, sinuous form, wings furled against its sides, claws sharp, scales just visible along its flanks and neck. Its head was long and narrow like a horse or a wolf, with bright eyes and scalloped ears above a mouth full of sharp teeth.

The girl clapped her hands. "Och, it's brilliant!" she told him. "Wait here!" And she was gone, racing back into the store. In her haste she'd left the coffeepot behind, and Knox helped himself to a refill, reasoning that she'd brought it outside for just that purpose.

A moment later she was back, this time dragging a man behind her. They had the same eyes, though his were in a wider, redder face still topped with the remains of dark red hair matching the tuft of a beard on his chin. He was laughing as they came to a stop by Knox.

"Apologies, sir," the man began. "But Edin here insists I see yer work. If yer willing, that is."

Knox merely turned the pad in reply, so they could both view the dragon there. "It's only a sketch," he explained. "And a quick one."

The man nodded. "Aye, an' yet it's a brilliant drawing, for all that," he said. "May I?" He gestured at the other chair, and with Knox's nod seated himself. "I'm Rory, Rory Travers, me wife Kate and I own this place. And ye've met ma daughter Edin already." The girl grinned behind him and held up a hand in greeting. "Ye're new here, aren't ye? Only, I've not seen ye around before, and I've lived me whole life here."

"Aye, just came to town recently," Knox admitted. "I'm working for Linda, over at the fish shop." He flipped back to the previous page, and Rory nodded at the drawing there.

"Right, right, she'd said she had some help." He tugged at his little beard. "Well, I'm no' wanting to steal ye away from her, but I'm wondering if ye'd take on a commission for us? Only, ye can see the outside's a tad plain, an' no' everyone can find us as a result. I'd been wanting to get a nice big sign, but Edin thinks we'd be better off with something more eye-catching. A mural, dontcha know, right along that wall there. Maybe something like yer dragon, only bigger and in color."

Knox glanced where he'd indicated. The wall was indeed a perfect canvas, and his pulse raced at the thought of covering it with his art. "I've never done anything that size before," he said, because he didn't want to lie to them. "And I've only ever worked in pencil and chalk. But I'd be more than happy to give it a go, if ye like. I'd need paints, though. And brushes."

Rory slapped the table, but not in anger. "Aye, we'd provide all ye needed," he agreed. "And pay ye for it, o' course." He named an amount, far more than Knox had made from Linda so far. "Ye could work on it on yer days off and such, if ye're willing." He grinned, glancing at Knox's cup. "And ye'd have free coffee and pastries, o' course, long as ye liked."

Knox found himself smiling back and offered his hand. "Ye've got yerself a deal."

Chapter Seven

Over the course of the next few weeks, Knox fell into a routine. Wake up with his alarm, shower, brush teeth—that had been strange but exciting, to feel his mouth so minty fresh!—dress, go downstairs and start the day. Work in the shop, with a quick break out back for lunch, until nearly dusk. Then head over to the café and work on the mural until it got too dark to see what he was doing.

He'd used his sketch as the rough outline, but transferring it to the wall had proven tricky, mainly because of the scale involved. Initially, he'd tried drawing it there with pencil as well, but those had proven useless on the whitewashed stone so he'd switched to a thick piece of charcoal. Once he'd roughed out the figure, Knox moved on to the next step, which was paint. He'd nearly wept with joy upon seeing all the vibrant colors the hardware store had to offer: greens and blues and yellows and reds, bright as any jewels, and all there for the taking. He'd settled on green and gold for the dragon itself, and blue for the sky behind, and Rory, who'd gone with him, had paid for the cans and brushes and helped lug them all back.

Originally, Knox had thought he'd paint each bit as he went, but he quickly realized that wouldn't work and had switched to filling in the dragon's full form first and then going back over it with details. It was taking shape, and already people were stopping by to admire it—and getting a coffee when they did. So that was working.

He'd also become friends with the Travers. They invited him to sup with them most nights. Sitting in their kitchen—their house was the one right beside the café, which was convenient—and sharing their talk and laughter made him ache for Elidh but also appreciate this strange new environment. Here people could interact without being mean or cruel, and conversation had nothing to do with hunting or killing and every-thing to do with work and customers and family and life in general.

Edin was eighteen, he learned, and recently done with school. She loved flowers, wanted a flower shop, and was always after her parents to let her try selling some of her garden's blooms at the café.

Rory was a kind, quiet man, given to bad puns and to singing random snatches from songs Knox had never heard but the others all groaned at. He was also the baker in the family, and all of the café's pastries came from him—"none of this 'farming it out to others' malarkey," he liked to say.

His wife, Kate, was louder, more assertive, but in a very mothering way. She fussed over Knox the very first time they met, exclaiming that he clearly didn't eat enough and doing her best to fix that. She was the one with the head for business and handled all of their budgeting and accounting.

And then there was Bram. He was six, a sturdy little lad not that much shorter than Knox, with his father's red hair and his mother's dark eyes and a bubbling little laugh you couldn't help but echo. He'd stared wide-eyed at Knox that first night, barely speaking, but by evening's end he was tugging Knox to his room to show off his stuffed animals and action figures.

There were a few younger Red Caps back at the castle, but Knox had never been close with any of them. They'd all been taught early on to despise him as much as the elders did, and to look down on him as a cross between a bad servant and a damaged relative. Bram's welcoming grin and sticky hello hugs brought tears to Knox's eyes every time.

When he finally finished the mural, Knox and the family stood outside on the patio to admire it.

"It's breathtaking," Kate declared, turning to engulf him in a big hug before going back to staring at the wall. "Absolutely fantastic."

"Aye, it's brilliant, like I knew it would be," Edin agreed, as she'd taken full credit for discovering him. Rory just nodded, but his full eyes and wide grin said it all without words. And Bram made them all laugh by dancing around them in a circle, shouting, "It's a dragon, we have our own dragon!"

"I guess that's that, then," Knox said after a time. He was bursting with pride over the mural—it really did look amazing, the dragon wind-ing its way among the clouds, its scales glowing in the same sunlight that tipped its claws with fire, its eyes alight, its teeth bared but something about its grin conveying not violence and malice but simply joy at being alive and in the air. At the same, Knox's heart was breaking. The job was done. His time with this wonderful family was at an end.

Rory must have been thinking something similar, because now he cleared his throat. "I've had a notion," he began slowly, scuffing a foot on the bricks. "The interior could use some freshening up too, aye? Nothing quite so grand as all this, there's no' enough space, but a fresh coat of paint and perhaps some small images here and there? Would ye be up for that, d'ya think?"

Knox's smile started slow, as comprehension dawned, and then spread so wide it nearly split his cheeks. "Oh, aye, I'm up for it." Edin smiled and gave him a quick sideways hug, and Kate engulfed him again, and Knox wondered if this was what it was like to have a real family, one that cared about you.

He was outside sketching designs for the bathroom walls a few days later when he heard a rhythmic tapping, then a shadow fell across his table. A man stood there, leaning on a silver-capped cane, his eyes upon the mural.

"I understand you are the artist responsible for this." His words were sharp, clipped, the accent unfamiliar, and Knox shaded his eyes to see more clearly. The man was tall and lean, with broad shoulders beneath an expensive-looking gray coat. His close-cropped hair was gray as well, and even his skin had a hard, grayish cast. That and his lined face made him look like he'd been carved from granite. Only his eyes stood out, being a dark, vibrant blue that nearly shone black. "It is fine work," the man continued. "Very, very fine."

"Thank ye. Yes, I painted it." All the village knew that, of course. Many had stopped in at Linda's to compliment Knox on his work, or said so to him when he was here. They didn't get that many out-of-towners, though, and none so conspicuously wealthy. Even the man's car, idling there at the curb, was obviously a luxury item, with its sweeping lines and silvery grille.

"I am called Herr vom Berge," the man introduced himself, clicking his heels together and executing a short bow before offering a gloved hand. "I was merely passing through on my way to Pittenweem—you are familiar with the Arts Festival there?"

"Knox Adair." Knox shook hands with him. "I've heard tell of it." He had, though only recently, but apparently it was considered a big deal in the region, second only to the Edinburgh Arts Festival for the quality and variety of work displayed. Edin had suggested he show his sketches there, but Knox couldn't fathom going so far from his new home.

The man, Herr vom Berge, smiled, a wintery expression. "I had not expected to find such beauty in such a place when I paused for a beverage. Tell me, are you available for commission, perhaps?"

Knox considered. "I might be," he allowed. Certainly, working on the mural had been both great fun and highly lucrative. It had never occurred to him before the mural that people might pay for his art. "But ye said ye were only passing through?"

"Indeed." Vom Berge inclined his head. "My home is in Karkonosze, in English they are called the Giant Mountains, you know of them?" At Knox's headshake, the man continued, "They are, hm, between Poland and the Czech Republic, yes." He smiled, briefly, as if at some private joke. "Though it was not always such." Then he waved that thought away, continuing, "My home there, it is too austere. It lacks color, life. I would fill it with art, the way you have done here. *Your* art, if you agree. Come work for me. I will make you very wealthy, and your paintings will enrich my home in return."

For a moment, Knox thought about it. The idea of an entire home — a mansion, from the sound of it — filled with his work? That would be amazing! But he'd seen a map or two now, thanks to Edin, and Poland was a long ways away. "Thank ye for the offer, truly," he said at last. "I'm good where I am, though." He had no desire to leave Kinglassie now that he'd finally started to feel at home here.

"Hm. Yes, I understand." Reaching into a coat pocket, vom Berge extracted a small silver case, from which he withdrew a sturdy card. "If you should change your mind," he explained, setting it down upon the table by Knox's cup. On the thick ivory cardstock was engraved his name and a number.

"Thanks." Knox took the card, savoring the feel of the paper, and pocketed it, then tipped his cap. "I won't, though."

"Indeed." Tapping his heels and bowing again, the man smiled. "Then I shall wish you good luck, and a good day." And, with that, he turned, his pivot sharp, and strode back to his car, which purred away a moment later.

It was a strange encounter, and Knox was flattered by the attention. But right now, he had a bathroom mural to finish sketching.

Chapter Eight

"Hullo? Anyone home?" Knox called as he slid open the glass rear door and stepped inside. It was dusk, and he was dining with the Travers again, but Linda'd had a shipment of fresh bass arrive after lunch and he'd stayed a little late to make sure all the new fish were properly prepared and iced. He'd hurried over right after, pausing only to collect a bottle of wine from the grocer's—it had become his habit to bring something, since Kate refused to let him share the costs of the meal, or help with the preparation. "Ye're our guest," she always said when he offered. "An' tha' means ye relax and enjoy." Edin occasionally huffed about "must be nice," but he could tell she was teasing when she said it.

Tonight, however, the little house was oddly dark and quiet. The café had shut an hour before and was clearly closed up for the night as he passed, so Edin and Rory should have had plenty of time to come home and wash up and help with laying the table and so on. Where was everyone?

Standing there, Knox took a deep whiff. He could smell food—chicken, he thought, and some sort of root vegetable—but the smell was harsh and bitter. Burnt. But Kate would never leave her stove unattended, especially not with Bram's curious little fingers around.

There was another smell, though, overlaid on that one, and it made Knox twitch as it filled his nostrils, overpowering all the rest. Rich, salty, almost cloying, it was a scent he'd hoped to never encounter again.

It was fresh blood. And not fish, which was far thinner and carried the tang of the sea. No, this was animal.

Or human.

Reversing the bottle in his grip so that he held it like a club, Knox moved deeper into the house. The table was already laid, he discovered, the empty plates and bowls staring up at him as he passed, a hint of his own face distorted in their weak reflections. The stove light was on, a single point in the dark, and he made his way in that direction.

His first step onto the tiled floor there squelched. And when he lifted his boot, it came up sticky, resisting his pull. At the same time, something dark thrummed through him. Dark and energizing.

His boots knew the taste of blood as well.

Kate lay there, her tall, broad form filling the narrow space between the lower cabinets. She was face down, which was a mercy, as either her head or chest had been caved in, judging from all the blood pooling about her. Her body was still cooling to the touch when Knox rested a shaking hand upon her shoulder.

She had not been dead for long.

"Rory?" He called as he rose, no longer caring whether he startled whoever'd done this. In fact, a part of him, an ugly part that looked like his father and elder siblings, welcomed the chance. Let them come. Let them see what happened when you angered a Red Cap.

But the rest of him, the larger part by far, was more concerned with finding the other Travers. "Rory?" he tried again. "Edin? Bram?"

Just past the kitchen, in the little hall leading to the bedrooms, he found Rory. The head of house was curled on his side, arms wrapped around his chest. His blood had soaked into the carpet, turning it black as pitch, and his eyes were wide and staring. Knox knelt and shut them before continuing on.

There were three bedrooms—a luxury, he'd thought upon seeing the place for the first time. The first one, the parents', was empty. So was the second, which was Edin's—only the scent of her flowers resided there.

The third and smallest was Bram's, and the door had been torn off its hinges, bashed in by some powerful blow. Too high for a kick, Knox's upbringing determined. A punch, or the blow from a shoulder.

The two younger Travers were huddled there, Edin encircling her brother in a vain attempt to shield him from the violence that had engulfed their family.

Knox could barely tell where one child stopped and the other started. Both were covered in their own blood, and mangled together, as if trapped in a vise that had crushed them into each other.

All he could be sure of was that they were dead and gone. And that the pain had been unimaginable.

For a moment, he knelt there beside them, head bowed, eyes closed, tears burgeoning behind his lids. They had been good people. Kind people. Kind to him. His first friends, practically his new family.

Who had done this to them, and why?

Brushing a hand over his face, Knox felt the streaks there and flinched. His hands were wet with their blood.

Sitting atop his head, his cap quivered like a leashed dog scenting a hare. Desperate for the blood so tantalizingly close.

With a growl, Knox straightened and stomped from the room, down the hall, into the dining room, well away from the bodies. "Never," he whispered to his hat. "Ye shall not have them!"

To prevent any further temptation, he stepped back outside. And, upon feeling his boots stick to the bricks there, glanced down.

He had tracked their blood all through the house and out onto the patio.

The Travers had a television—something else Knox had never seen before coming here. After dinner most nights, they'd invited him to stay and watch their shows with them. One was a police drama. Thinking back on that now, Knox could picture how this might go:

Local family is murdered. New arrival in town often dined with them. His footprints are all over the scene. And, if questioned, the police learn that he has no ID. No history. And no alibi.

He had to get out of here.

There was a hose for watering the plants, and Knox hurried over to that, turning the faucet and then directing the water toward his feet, clearing any trace of blood from his soles. Then, switching that back off, he rushed back to Linda's. Maybe if he claimed to not have made it over for dinner yet? She could confirm that he'd stayed to work late tonight.

But when he reached the fish shop, Knox knew something was wrong here as well. The front door was ajar. Linda would have locked up when she left—she'd only stayed behind to transfer the fish to coolers.

He pushed the door open—and it shuddered to a stop halfway, unable to move past an obstacle there.

An obstacle that had, less than an hour ago, told him, "Go on, get. I've got the rest."

Linda stared up at the ceiling, seeing none of it, nothing of the place she'd built herself and run on her own for many years. The side of her head had been crushed, blood and hair and flesh and bone all matted together.

She had died quickly, at least. A single blow and she'd been gone.

Though she hadn't been the kindest of souls, she'd been good to him, and Knox mourned her nearly as much as the Travers.

Then he saw more of that police drama unfold in his head. Newcomer works at the local fish shop. Someone just killed its owner, same night as the family died. He's got no alibi for either one.

It was an open-and-shut case, as they called it. And Knox would be lucky to get life in prison. Which could either be a few weeks if he didn't wet his cap or a few centuries if he somehow did.

Either way, he was done for. His only chance was to run.

Skirting around Linda's body, Knox raced upstairs to his room. When he'd first arrived, he'd discovered that Linda had left some things in the space's small closet, including a battered old rucksack. Now he stuffed his clothes and toiletries into that, along with his sketchpad and drawing supplies. What little cash he had was already in his pocket. He considered emptying the register, but that would only make him look more guilty. Besides, the faster he left, the better.

So much for his nice, normal new life.

Exiting the fish shop for the last time, Knox took a second to glance back up at it. His first real home. He'd hoped it would last forever.

Then he resolutely turned his back on that and quickly marched down the road.

A few miles away, Knox stopped at a petrol station to determine his next step. Where should he go? Anywhere but here, obviously, but that was too big, too vague. He needed a destination. A plan.

He'd bought a coffee on reflex, but raising it to his lips made him think of Edin handing him a cup at the café, smiling and laughing and asking to see his latest sketches. With a grimace, Knox set the cup down and pushed it away. Never again.

Something in his pocket jabbed him as he shifted, and he drew it out with a frown. That man's business card. It had only been yesterday, but the recent horrors had driven it entirely from his mind. Now, though, Knox turned the card over and over, considering.

What did he have to lose?

The station was old-fashioned enough to still have a row of pay phones outside. Knox went to the nearest, dropping in a few coins and dialing the number on the card. A moment later, there was a *click*.

"Yes?" It was definitely the same man.

"Herr vom Berge? This is Knox Adair. We met the other day, in Kinglassie. About painting murals in your home. I wondered if the offer was still open?" It all came out in a rush.

There was a second's pause. "Yes, I recall," came the dry voice at last. "Yes, it is still open. I have just finished here in Pittenweem, and shall be departing for home at dawn from Dundee Airport. You know where that is?"

"I can find it," Knox promised. There were maps at the counter inside.

"Very well. I shall see you at dawn." And, with a click, the man ended the call.

Dundee Airport. Knox sighed as he hung up the receiver and turned back toward the station interior. Probably not close by, or he'd have heard of it.

Looked like he'd be running tonight. But at least he had a plan. And wearing himself out physically might help keep him from seeing the Travers' torn, broken bodies every time he closed his eyes.

CHAPTER NINE

THE TREK WAS INDEED A LONG ONE, SOME FORTY MILES OR SO, HE GUESSED, with parts of it over rough terrain, but Knox channeled all of his grief into motion, which gave him energy to burn. He reached the airport well before midnight.

He had nearly gotten used to cars at this point, and even trucks, but the sight of a vehicle swooping down from above like some enormous bird made Knox freeze like a mouse sighting an owl. Then it passed overhead, coming to a stop along the wide runway beyond with an audible bump, and he was able to breathe again. But was that what he would soon be riding in? He wasn't sure he'd be able to bear it.

A large chain-link fence surrounded the airport, and a beefy security guard stood in a little booth beside the one gate. "Help ye, lad?" he asked, leaning out to look Knox over. If his tone was not completely unfriendly it wasn't exactly welcoming, either.

"Uh, yeah, hiya," Knox replied, clutching the strap of his rucksack. "Uh, I'm supposed ta meet Herr vom Berge here. At dawn. For a flight. And a job."

At the sound of the gentleman's name, the guard straightened, sucking in his gut like he was on parade. "Oh! Ye'd be Knox Adair, then? I've get ye on me list." Without even waiting for a reply, he hit a button. The gate clicked and started sliding open all on its own. "Hangar One, that'd be. Ye can wait there, no worries at all."

"Thanks." Relieved that he was being allowed in after all—and that the guard hadn't asked to see any ID—he hurried through the opening. There were several large buildings he guessed were hangars, all off to one side of the long runway. Each had a number painted on the side and also set above the broad double doors. The doors to the first hangar were already open, so Knox headed on in.

The plane he'd just seen land had been a little thing, with a propeller on the front and red stripes along the top-mounted wings and the side.

The one sitting in Hangar One made that thing look like a toy. An old, outdated toy.

It was sleek and shiny, and all silver except for a tasteful gray stripe down its side. It had no propeller blunting its coned front, and its wings rose from underneath in a graceful backward sweep. There were windows all along the side, spaced around an oval door, currently shut.

The hangar itself was a big, open space, roughly as large at the great hall back home. It was all gray and white, with a plain concrete floor and corrugated metal walls that curved up to form the ceiling high above. Bright rows of lights hung from metal beams, keeping the space noon-bright even at this hour. Toward the back Knox spied several tall metal cabinets, a few long tables, and some chairs, presumably where the people who worked on the plane might keep their tools and take breaks. No one was around, so Knox claimed one of the chairs, dropping his rucksack on the ground beside him and propping his feet on the nearest table. Then, the exertions and shocks of the day finally catching up to him, he tugged his cap down over his eyes and fell asleep.

Knox woke from a dream of a blood-soaked Edin begging him to save her when something tapped him on the shoulder. It wasn't a hand, but something narrower and harder. Blinking, he saw it was the silver head of a dark wooden cane.

"Good morning, Mister Adair," his new employer stated with another of those odd clicking bows. "I am pleased that you are here, and so punctual, yes?"

"Ah, yeah, sorry," Knox answered, returning his feet to the ground and rubbing his eyes as he sat up, shoving all thoughts about recent tragedies aside as best he could. "I came straight here, and the guard said it'd be okay for me to wait inside." He rose and hefted his rucksack, doing his best to focus on the present and future rather than the immediate past. "I'm all good to go, though."

"Excellent." Vom Berge did not appear to be offended by his new employee's having slept in the hangar. "My preparations are also complete, and so we may depart as soon as the plane is ready." He gestured, and Knox saw that the aircraft's door stood open, with a small set of steps leading up to it. "Shall we?"

Knox followed the tall man across the hangar, noticing as he did that some men in coveralls were loading a handful of wide but flat wooden boxes into the plane's rear compartment. "What are those?"

"Oh, I made a few purchases at the Art Festival," vom Berge replied. "They will go very nicely in the study, I am thinking." A young woman in a dark skirt and matching jacket waited at the top of the stairs and stepped aside to let them enter the plane, smiling at them both. Knox wasn't sure what he'd been expecting, exactly, but this thickly carpeted, wood-paneled chamber wasn't it. Large, comfortable leather chairs were stationed on either side, with small tables affixed to the walls between them. Sconces gave the space a cheery glow, and curtains covered the windows, cutting down the glare from the hangar lights. It felt like a narrow but posh living room, if a slightly chilly one.

"Please, make yourself comfortable anywhere," vom Berge told him, claiming a seat toward the back. "Facilities are near the front, and there is a kitchen as well — once we are underway, you may ask the chef for anything you'd like." He then directed his attention to the young woman. "Suzette, please inform the captain that we may depart at his earliest convenience."

She nodded and hurried forward, poking her head through a doorway at the far end as Knox selected a chair and sank into its thick cushions. It was the most comfortable thing he'd ever sat in.

That didn't change the fact that he was nervous about flying, though. To distract himself, he asked, "Will this take us right to your home?" He had no idea if that was even a thing, but since Herr vom Berge was clearly wealthy he thought it might be.

The man gave him a dry smile in return. "Alas, no," he answered. "My estate is too remote and the ground too uneven and rocky for a runway. We will fly into Pardubice Airport. That is in the Czech Republic. My private railcar is ready at the station there to take us to Karpacz, in Poland. My driver will be waiting for us when we arrive, and we will drive the rest of the way up into Karkonosze. I live upon Wielki Szyszak, the highest peak of the western range." He uttered a short, sharp laugh. "It is a long way to travel, with many steps. But to me it is worth it. I would not abandon my home for anything, and I enjoy my privacy, yet I cannot resist seeing the rest of the world and admiring the great art it has to offer. And, when I am very fortunate, I am able to bring some of that same art home with me."

"Oh. Uh, cool." Knox knew he probably sounded like an idiot. Maybe he was. This guy traveled the world, just to see and buy art! That was amazing! Knox had grown up someplace just as remote as this estate sounded, but no one in his family ever left it except to hunt, or to steal. Even then, they never went far from the loch and its surroundings. He was the first to leave the region — and soon he'd be leaving the country completely!

If only Elidh could see me now, he thought. But that thought was immediately followed by another, far more tragic one:

Edin would have loved this.

He was saved from his own spiraling emotions by a sudden jolt as the entire cabin lurched forward, then began picking up speed, the wind whistling past outside. "You have never flown before?" Herr vom Berge asked, watching him closely. At Knox's frantic headshake, the man smiled. "You may wish to close your eyes this first time, and to grip the arms of the chair. It is all perfectly safe, I assure you, but it can feel alarming to the uninitiated."

Knox did as instructed — but even so, he felt his stomach drop and his head spin as the plane's motion went from rushing forward to lifting upward. There was no mistaking that sudden ascent, either, as the very air pushed Knox down into his seat, squashing the breath from his chest. Fortunately, that passed after a moment, and he blinked and glanced out the window.

And wished he hadn't.

They were so high up already! The ground had fallen away below, the hangars and runways already the size of model toys, and clouds rushed past as they continued to soar up, up into the sky. It felt as if they might crash into the sun!

But then the plane leveled out, and Knox was able to relax a little bit, at least enough to unclench his fingers where they dug into the chair arms. The sky above was a perfect, peaceful blue. The sun shone brightly. The clouds just below them formed a fleecy blanket of soft whites and grays. Even the motion didn't seem as severe, though he could see that they were in fact traveling at phenomenal speed.

A small chime sounded somewhere. "We have attained what is referred to as cruising altitude," Herr vom Berge explained. "This is good. It will be a smooth ride now." He waved Suzette over. "A glass of the Malbec, please, and some scones with that gooseberry preserve, I think. Would you care for anything, Mr. Adair?"

Knox started to shake his head, then realized that he was in fact ravenous. He hadn't eaten last night, though he quickly pushed that realization aside. "Uh, yeah, something'd be great, thanks. Whatever's easy. Breakfast, I guess? And tea. Please. Thanks."

Suzette dipped her head. "Of course." When she returned a short while later, she had an entire English breakfast on a tray for him, which she set down on the little table at his chair. "Let me know if you'd like anything else."

Digging into the food, Knox thought that, if this was any indication what working for Herr vom Berge would be like, he might be very happy he'd kept that card. And right now, he suspected a complete change of scenery would do him good.

CHAPTER TEN

THE TRIP WENT EXACTLY AS HERR VOM BERGE—WHO TOLD KNOX HE could also "call me Lord John" with that odd twist of the lip that suggested some sort of private joke—had outlined it. The plane ride took three hours and Knox had almost begun to relax and get used to the idea of being thousands of feet in the air and moving at several hundred kilometers an hour when they'd started their descent, which had him clutching the chair arms all over again. Somehow the last minute or two, once they had touched down, actually seemed worse, despite the fact that they were probably going slower by then, but he survived it. He was also a little woozy, he guessed from the air travel, and so was perfectly content to just follow after his new employer, who clearly knew exactly where he was going and who had officials falling all over themselves to assist him along the way.

By comparison, the train ride from there to Poland was nothing. It took nearly as much time as the plane ride had but Herr vom Berge's private car was even fancier than his jet's cabin. Knox spent most of the ride asleep in one of the big, overstuffed armchairs there, a thick blanket tucked around him to fend off the cold that pervaded the space. Once they'd reached Karpacz they exited the train and climbed into a large luxury vehicle, the kind that was as big as a truck but far nicer than any car, and headed up into the mountains. They set out at dawn and pulled up at the manor's imposing front gates a little past noon.

"Welcome to Berghaus," Lord John declared as the heavy metal gates parted and the car passed slowly through the widening gap. "That means 'Mountain Home' in German."

Knox nodded, a bit fuzzy-headed and too busy taking everything in to answer. The gates had to be at least three times his height, and the thick stone pillars supporting them were even taller. Beyond that was a long, winding drive through thick snow, and past that—

He stared.

Knox had grown up in a castle, albeit a ruined one. He was familiar with stone structures, and grand ones at that. This was something else.

The house, such as it was, was built *into* the side of a mountain.

The mountain rose up ahead of them, a seemingly unbroken slab of rock, nearly vertical, that stretched up and up and up until it abruptly cut off like it had been sheared away by some titanic blade. But carved into its base directly before them was the front of an enormous, palatial home, complete with tall, turreted rooms jutting out in a cluster at both ends and a wide, arched porch sheltering a set of enormous double doors made of some dark wood or metal or stone and heavily carved in fanciful designs. Tall windows ran down either side, three rows of them, indicating the stories concealed within, and though Knox suspected each window was taller than even their master, they looked tiny against the scale of the house and, beyond that, the enormity of the mountain.

The car pulled up before those doors and Knox and Lord John exited the car. Several men and women had already bustled from the house and now collected the boxed artwork and a few pieces of luggage from the boot, while Knox refused the offer to have them take his rucksack. In this strange setting, that was one of the only familiar notes, so he clung to it.

"Ah, Gerta," Lord John said, addressing a beefy woman with graying blonde hair who had approached with the rest but stood back as they handled the unpacking. "This is Knox Adair, my new mural painter. Please set him up with quarters and whatever else he needs." He glanced at Knox. "Once you are settled, I will show you where I would like you to begin."

Knox nodded and let himself be led away by Gerta, whose manner was brusque just shy of rude. She led him into the house, down the wide main hall and then off to a smaller side hall, up a narrow flight of stairs, and to a door that opened onto a set of rooms. Knox couldn't have said how they'd gotten here, or where here was in relation to the front doors or anything else.

"These will be yours," Gerta told him. "Supper will be at six. Luncheon is at noon. Breakfast is at six in the morning." Then she exited, leaving him alone to explore this strange new place.

There were three rooms in all: a front room with couches and chairs and a fireplace, a small side room with a desk and chair, and a bedroom with bed, dresser, and nightstand. He also had his own bathroom, with both a sunken tub and a step-down standing shower. The bathroom floor and walls were all marble, but even with their more familiar wooden floors the entire suite felt… cold. Expensive, even luxurious, but cold.

He dropped his rucksack on the bed, poked through each room, then took the door back out into the hall. Having no idea where to go from there, Knox began to wander. There seemed an almost endless supply of rooms, each one different and all with that same chilly elegance, and for at least an hour he opened this door and that, never running across another living soul. What he did find were the kind of spaces he'd only seen on the Travers' TV before now: a library, stuffed with books all the way to the ceiling, most not in English; a game room, with a billiards table, a dart board, a chess set, and a felt-covered octagonal table with eight chairs; an indoor swimming pool, the water clear as crystal, blue as the sky, and cold as ice; a portrait gallery, lined on one side with images of people who looked nothing like Herr vom Berge and on the other with paintings that either were him or were direct ancestors who looked just like him; a room with thick pads on the floor, possibly for exercise though there wasn't any equipment in it; a comfortable room with reclining seats set in rows and a large screen at the far end, though Knox saw no way to work it; several bedrooms; several bathrooms; two rooms that could have been studies, each with a large desk and matching chair; and, at last, a staircase leading down.

He had only descended a few steps when someone peeked up from below. "Mister Adair?" the unfamiliar man called. "If you'd follow me, Lord John is waiting for you in the great room."

Relieved to know he was not alone in this place, and to find someone who knew where he should go and how to get there, Knox hurried down. The speaker proved to be of middle age, average height, and a slightly rotund shape. He did not smile or return Knox's hello, instead turning and immediately leading down a different corridor.

Knox followed along, quickly abandoning any attempt to engage the man. He clearly knew his way around, though, and a few minutes later Knox was being shown into the great room.

Immediately, he saw that the space suited its name. It was easily thrice the length of his entire suite, and possibly more, while its ceilings stretched far overhead. Massive beams marched along across the ceiling, seeming pencil-thin from this distance. An enormous fireplace of some dark wood took up much of the far end, its thick mantle handsome and heavy, though the hearth was cold and dark. The floor was beautifully inlaid parquet and the walls — the walls were off-white and plain as could be.

Lord John waited by that empty fireplace. "Ah, Mister Adair," he started, turning as Knox approached. "Very good. I trust that your rooms are satisfactory? Excellent. Now, this will be your first project here. As you can see, the room does not lack decoration or detail — except on the walls. They are hideous. Please exercise your art to make them beautiful. Gerta will provide whatever materials you need, and you should feel free to go with whatever design aesthetic you feel works best. I merely wish for something that enhances the space's natural beauty, draws the eye to its features, and then steals some of that same attention for itself. Does that provide you sufficient detail to begin?"

Studying the space, Knox nodded slowly. "Aye, I can work with that," he agreed, rubbing his chin. "At least enough to sketch something. Then ye can see if ye like it or no'. If it's a no, I'll revise or toss it out and start again. If it's a yes, we're good to move on to Step Two."

His new employer nodded. "Very good. I will leave you to it, then. Gerta already informed you of the meal schedule, yes? Lunch will be served very soon. I hope you like your roast beef rare." He stalked off, cane tapping his progress across the floor, before Knox had time to reply.

Still, he was already getting too caught up in the project to mind. This was essentially a set of enormous and interconnected blank canvases, four of them, five with the ceiling. Knox considered, letting ideas play out in his head. He'd only recently graduated to paints, and to large surfaces. Now he had the chance to work on a scale he'd never even imagined before. There were so many things he wanted to try!

Best to keep it simple, though. Without any help, he could be at this one room for months, even years. Especially if he didn't get it just right the first time. He had the feeling Lord John — Herr vom Berge — was going to be a very particular client indeed.

Then again, that might be exactly what he needed right now. Someone exacting to force him into staying busy, and into putting in his best effort. Knox knew he'd relive the horror of finding the Travers for years to come, but at least if he lost himself in paint colors and brush strokes and palettes and motifs it might not hurt so much.

That was what he was hoping, anyway.

Chapter Eleven

For the first few days, Knox did indeed throw himself into the work. He sketched several possible designs in his pad, but wound up discarding each one: too complicated, too busy, too garish, too monotone, too static. Nothing seemed to fit.

Part of the problem, he realized, was that he didn't know where to start. Not in terms of the actual physical location, that was simple enough — it made the most sense to start at the room's far end, to one side of the doors, and then wrap around and end back at the doors again. No, the problem was that he didn't know enough about his host and patron to have a sense of what he might like, what would fit not only the architecture but his personal style and taste. Did the man love dragons? Did he loathe them? Did he enjoy nature scenes, or find those too prosaic? Did he love the color purple or despise any shade of red? And despite having said to "do whatever you feel fits best," it still felt like there was a "as long as I like it" caveat hovering just behind that. So how to know what those likes were?

Knox would simply have to find out.

He could ask, of course, but he actually hadn't seen Lord John since they'd arrived. That first lunch had been served in an enormous dining room, as cold as the rest of the manor, with only the two of them present at opposite ends of a leagues-long table. That had proven advantageous, as the roast beef had indeed been rare, and given the distance between them and his host's apparent focus on his own food Knox had felt only a little awkward about taking his cap off and dipping it quickly in the juices pooling on his plate. His cap had become almost dry despite it having been only a few days since its last immersion at the fish shop, and returning the cap to his head had cleared his thoughts immediately, as well as banishing much of what he'd thought to be mere travel fatigue. But for the evening meal Knox had been told that "the master has opted to dine in his room, and we can bring yours to your quarters as well."

Not much liking the idea of eating alone in such a grand and forbidding place, Knox instead asked, "Kin I no' eat with you lot?"

Gerta, who had been the one informing him of all this, appeared taken aback. "You wish to dine with the staff?" Her tone made it clear she did not approve.

But Knox nodded nonetheless. "Aye, I'm more staff than guest, I'd say," he pointed out. "An' I'm no' a fan of eating alone."

"Hm." She considered, and though her nod was grudging it was at least a nod. "Yes, very well. You may join us in the kitchens if you wish."

So that night Knox went down there instead, finding a wide, thick-beamed room warm from the cookfire in the broad stone fireplace and cheery with its sturdy wooden furniture and the bright colors of vegetables and tubers and fruits everywhere. He wound up having a far friendlier meal with the place's surprisingly small staff, which consisted of: Gerta herself; Hans the head butler, who had been the one to guide Knox to the great hall that first day; Rolf the cook and Liesel his wife, assistant, and pastry chef; Danika the maid; Karl the groundskeeper; and Miche the dogsbody. Most of them had been welcoming right from the start, and even Gerta had mostly warmed to him by meal's end as he told the tale of his first terrifying time in an airplane.

After that, Knox took all of his meals in the kitchen, happy to spend time with people in the only warm space he'd found yet. All of them seemed nice enough, and so after those first few days he took advantage of that to ask about their mutual employer. "I'm just trying ta get a sense o' what he likes," he explained. "So I kin tell what kinda art'll appeal."

"Oh, the master enjoys all forms of art, really," Hans was quick to offer. "I'm sure anything you do, he will like. He did hire you, after all, so he trusts your vision."

"His collection has a lot of variety," Danika agreed. "Landscapes, portraits, still lifes, maps, all sorts."

"And not just paintings," Miche added. "There's the sculptures, as well. They're everywhere."

"He's been collecting his whole life," was Gerta's contribution. "Hans is right, there is little he does not like in the way of art."

"Hm." That, unfortunately, didn't help much, so Knox tried a different tack. "This place is grand, but cold, aye? So, I'm thinking perhaps an autumnal scene, trees in full color, leaves falling in sunset, that sort of thing?"

Liesel clapped her hands together. "Oh, that'd be lovely!" She was a cheerful sort, given to such expressions. "I am sure he would adore it."

The others all nodded, and so it was settled. Yet Knox felt like he knew little more about Herr vom Berge than he had before.

"This house is old, yeah?" he asked Miche after they'd all eaten and people were splitting off to return to their duties or head to their own rooms for the night—the staff had most of one wing, he'd learned. "Must be a century old, or more?"

The older man nodded. He had that grizzled look of someone who spent a good deal of time outdoors. "Yes, my father worked here before me, and his before him." Like the other staff, he had a strong, sharp accent, the words all bitten off at their ends.

"So, Lord John's grandfather, then?" But Knox was surprised at the man's answering frown.

"Naw, far as I know it's been him the whole time."

"That's... unusual, isn't it?" He had to ask, because he still wasn't entirely sure. His own kind lived several centuries, but he didn't think that was typical for humans.

Miche shrugged. "Guess so. Never asked."

The next day, Knox broached the subject with Liesel. "Oh, the lord's family is very long-lived," she replied cheerfully. "Everyone in the area knows that."

"How long-lived are we talking?" Knox asked her. "Not as old as the house, surely?"

She just shrugged and laughed. "I never heard of anyone else living here before him, but who knows?"

That afternoon, Knox went back up to the picture gallery—by now he'd learned enough to navigate through the main wing and to and from his own rooms, at least. He focused on the portraits all along the left side, the ones that looked like Herr vom Berge. He'd initially thought those had to be ancestors.

But were they? Or were they all portraits of him, instead? If so, they stretched back hundreds of years. Longer even than Clan Adair's Matriarch.

That couldn't be normal.

That led Knox to wonder about some other things. He'd thought Lord John's coloring was simply a lack of sunlight or some sort of hereditary condition—he still wasn't all that familiar with people in all their variety. He'd yet to see anyone else so rigorously, thoroughly gray. So stonelike. Between that and the cold and the question of longevity—

Was Herr vom Berge even human?

But if he wasn't, what was he? Knox didn't know anything about any race besides humans and Red Caps. He'd heard tales of others, though, enough to be sure they weren't alone in the world. Which didn't help him much in this case.

One of the things in Knox's room was a television. That he'd seen at the Travers', though this one was as thin as a slim book, as large as a landscape, and so vivid it felt like he was there. It also had hundreds of channels, so many he'd yet to flip through them all.

Another thing, sitting on the desk in the little study, was a computer. Knox had seen one of those at the Travers' as well, but had never tried operating one himself. He'd watched Edin, though, when she'd wanted to show him several new flowers she'd planned to try growing. He quickly shut those memories down and concentrated on the machine instead. After a few tries, he got it turned on, and with a bit of fumbling he got the little arrow on the screen to move where he wanted.

Then he clicked an image along the bottom, and what opened looked a lot like the screen he'd seen Edin using. There was a space there to type something, just as she had.

Knox typed in "Herr vom Berge."

The screen changed at once, to show a list of entries. Like an encyclopedia. Interesting. The first few looked to be business articles, though he couldn't be sure because they weren't in English. Several more were from some sort of local paper, like the ones he'd seen back in Kinglassie, and though they were not in English either Knox suspected they were the equivalent of "local man funds parade" or "leading citizen pays for road repaving."

But at the very bottom of the list, he spotted something else. Something about an old German poem. And there was an option to translate it to English.

He clicked that.

And read with growing horror.

Chapter Twelve

That night, Knox went looking for his employer.

"He is dining alone again," Gerta informed him when he asked. "As, in fact, is his usual. That first lunch with you was, I believe, an attempt to put you at ease here."

"Well, I've no desire to eat with him again, so that's fine," Knox told her, more sharply than perhaps was warranted. "But I do need to be speaking with him about something of some importance."

The housekeeper tapped her lower lip but finally nodded. "I can convey that request."

"Thank ye."

He wasn't expecting anything to come of that, necessarily, so was both surprised and pleased when she found him in the great hall not long after and said, "the master will see you in his study, if you please."

That was a room Knox had not yet visited, and in fact an entire wing he had not seen, as she led him up a set of narrow, winding stone stairs to a tall, thin door of such dark wood it was nearly black. A massive iron knocker adorned the front, and she pounded that once before turning the knob and stepping back to let Knox slip by.

"Ah, Mister Adair," Herr vom Berge said as he entered. "I trust you have found everything to your liking thus far? Accommodations satisfactory? Food acceptable? Any other immediate needs met?" He was sitting in a high-backed leather chair behind a massive desk that filled much of the small, octagonal room. Directly behind him was a tall, arched window looking out upon the bleak landscape below and open to allow a biting wind to curl through, and the other walls were covered in paintings above and sculptures below. It was like a large art gallery had been packed into the tiny space.

"Yes, well, abut tha'," Knox began. He crossed the room and stopped just shy of the desk. "I dinna think ye've been entirely straight with me, eh?" He crossed his arms over his chest. "Yer name, it'd no' rightly be Herr vom Berge, would it? Or Lord John neither? It'd more properly be... Rübezahl?"

The effect of that one word was immediate. His host seemed to swell, growing larger until his head and shoulders blocked the window, casting the room into shadow. His skin darkened as well, and grew rougher, more like the stone outside, while his eyes began to glow with a sharp blue light.

Then, after such a brief time Knox almost wondered if he'd imagined it, the fearsome figure before him unclenched. Light returned, and once again Knox faced a tall, lean man with a grayish cast to his features.

"I do not care for that name," his host declared sharply. "It was first said in jest—no, in ridicule—and I will not answer to it. I prefer the names I have given you instead, if you please."

"But ye *are* him?" Knox pressed. "The mountain spirit? Sometimes a giant, and ye bring lightning and storms down on people?" *And murder those who cross ye*, he added but managed not to say. Yet.

Lord John nodded. "I have been known to do so, yes, but only when it was warranted," he admitted slowly. "Where did you learn of this?"

"There's a poem," Knox answered. "I found it online. But it was the portraits that gave ye away. And the fact that no one here can ever remember ye not being here."

That brought a thin smile to the man's face. "Indeed. But surely my true nature is not a problem for one such as you? For you are not of the mundane yourself." The smile became a grin, showing surprisingly long and sharp teeth, like a wolf's. "Unless the folk of Scotland often require blood for their headwear?"

"Ah." Knox took off the cap in question, clutching it in both hands. "Ye noticed that, did ye?"

"Naturally. It is why I requested rare beef for that lunch. Air travel tends to dry one out. *Jus* is not quite the same as true blood, of course, but I hoped it would suffice."

That explained it, and Knox couldn't fault his employer for thinking of him. But he still had to reconcile that with what he'd read—and, worse, what he'd begun to suspect. "So ye know what I am, then. And now I know what ye are, as well. Are there others here?"

"Other Red Caps?" Lord John actually chuckled at his own little joke. "No, you are the only one of your kind I have been acquainted with. That was part of the appeal to hiring you, I must admit. Could others have murals hand-painted in their homes? Yes, of course, though each would be unique. But could anyone else have a mural painted by a Red Cap? No, only I. And as a collector, I appreciate that distinction a great deal." He tapped the fingers of one hand upon the desk, drumming them in rhythm as he thought. "I admit that I had heard tales of your clan, but everything I know of them suggests you may well be the first to travel beyond the British Isles. As for whether there is another like me, there are none, alas. Or, if there are, they have kept themselves well hidden, and I have no wish to invade their privacy, any more than I would wish them to intrude on mine. Or did you simply mean other supernaturals?" He shook his head. "The members of my staff are all human. I have encountered others over the years, here and there, but infrequently, and none who would consent to work for me even if I were to ask."

Knox nodded, trying his best to sound casual though his heart felt like a hummingbird trapped in his chest. "And the murdering and rampaging and all that? Is that still a thing for ye?"

"Would it matter if it was?" the master of the house asked. "It would not affect you any, nor the task for which you were hired. But no. As I said, I only did such things when it was merited by previous actions on those people's part, or necessitated by some other need. I have mellowed significantly over the years. My emphasis is on collecting and preserving art now, as I told you when we first met."

Knox scowled. "Some other need, aye? Tha' sounds ominous, it does."

The smile he received in return was all bared teeth. "When I set my mind upon something, Mister Adair, it is folly to oppose me," Lord John stated. "For there is little I will not do to achieve it." That *did* sound threatening. And hinted at exactly what Knox had feared since reading those details online. "Do we have a problem?" the man—or spirit—asked next, with a noticeable bite to those words.

That tone made Knox realize the danger he was in, and cast about for a way out. "I'd have preferred to know yer nature afore we left me homeland," he said slowly, mind racing. "But me own kin're known for their bloody ways, and I'd no' want ta be judged by their actions." He donned his cap once more. "Tha's all."

"Excellent. Because I would hate for you to attempt reneging upon our agreement," Lord John told him bluntly. "That would be… unfortunate. Not to mention difficult for you, given our isolated location."

"Right." Knox backed up a step, then another. "Well, glad ta know, at least. I'll leave ye to it." And he hurried from the room.

Once outside, the hall almost feeling warm by comparison, Knox pressed his back to the wall. For the first time since leaving Castle Lachlan, he was afraid—not of some great unknown, but of actual physical attack.

From his new employer, an ancient, malevolent mountain spirit. Who now had him trapped in a remote castle high in the mountains.

Knox shivered, his knees going weak.

He had turned the man down initially. Said he was happy where he was.

Then the Travers had died. Horribly murdered, for no apparent reason. And Linda as well. Leaving him with no friends, no employer, no home, the police potentially coming for him, and nowhere to go.

Nowhere but here.

He sagged down onto the top step and huddled there, gasping for breath. Lord John—no, call him by the right name for such an atrocity, Rübezahl—had killed them. That much was blindingly clear now. That creature in there had slaughtered them all. Just to trick Knox into coming here.

"No one else has a mural painted by a Red Cap." Those words rose up and threatened to choke Knox. Because of course someone else *had.* The Travers. But not anymore—because they were all dead.

Edin and Bram, Rory and Kate, even Linda—dead because of him. Because he'd said no to a being that made his own kin look like veritable angels, a creature who had not only wanted Knox's art but wanted to be the sole possessor of such.

And now he was working for that man—that monster. Stuck here with him. Unable to escape, and unable to say no.

What the hell was he going to do?

Chapter Thirteen

Gathering his resolve, Knox lurched to his feet and half-stumbled, half-ran down the steps. Then along the corridor to the main hall, and out the front door.

The cold air shocked his system, even after the chill of the manor, but Knox welcomed it. It stripped away the fog of uncertainty and the shroud of grief — and fear. He needed to get out of here, and right away. That much was obvious. He could figure out the rest later.

Each breath was like a knife, slicing through his chest, and in nothing but jeans, T-shirt, and flannel, Knox was frozen after only a few steps. But he didn't stop. Instead, he let his fear and rage and sorrow propel him forward, until he slammed into the front gates.

They were shut, of course. He yanked on one side, tugging with all his strength, but it didn't even rattle. It wasn't just locked, it was latched tight.

"Hoy, do not do that!" It was Miche, hurrying toward him from the house. "The master will not like it!"

Knox ignored the warning, pulling at the gate again, but it was no use. Even at full strength he doubted he'd be able to budge it. Instead, he turned as the dogsbody approached. "I need out, Miche. Please, open the gate. Could you? For me?"

The older man frowned, his furrowed brow only just visible beneath his thick fur hat and above the collar of his heavy, lined coat. "I am sorry, my friend. I cannot. It would be my job. And worse. Why you need out so badly? You want something? We get it for you!"

"Yes," Knox answered, desperately grasping at that. "I do want something. Paints! I need paints! But I need to go with you into town, to be able to pick out the ones I need!" He could slip away in town. True, he'd still be in another country, with no money and no friends and not even speaking the language—he'd heard several people talking on the trip up here and couldn't make heads nor tails of it—but it would be a start.

But Miche was already shaking his head. "I no leave either, except in the master's car," he explained. "And only to drive him or fetch him back from a trip. We will tell Bartosz what you need. He will bring it."

"Bartosz?" Knox thought he knew everyone here by now—there weren't many at Berghaus, after all. "Who's that?"

"He lives in the village," Miche answered. "He brings out deliveries. Once a week."

"Oh." That was something, anyway. "When's he coming next?" Knox hoped the man hadn't just been—he wasn't sure he could handle pretending to like being here for another week.

Fortunately, Miche smiled. "Two days," he said. "Wednesday. You have a list, Gerta will give it to him then."

Two days. Well, that wasn't long. Knox nodded. "Okay. Thanks." He turned back toward the house but changed his mind after a second. "You go on ahead," he told Miche. "I need to clear my head."

The man slapped him on the back. "Yes, brisk mountain air good for that." But he wasted no time returning to the heated hall himself, leaving Knox alone outside. Good. As soon as the front door had shut, Knox returned to the gates—but this time, instead of trying to force them open, he grabbed hold of the handles and used them to haul himself up, wedging the toes of his boots into the spaces just above the gate's thick bottom lip. If he couldn't open the stupid things barring his path, maybe he could climb them instead.

As a small child, Knox had climbed the stones of the old castle with his siblings and cousins. They'd climbed the few small, stunted trees nearby, as well. But that had been years ago. He'd been younger, quicker.

And not wearing massive iron boots.

The gates didn't have any significant protrusions anywhere. And the handles were too high for Knox to leap onto them. He scrambled to pull himself higher somehow, but just kept sliding back down.

Abandoning the attempt, he paced to the right. Maybe the walls themselves would offer more purchase? But though the stone blocks were rough-cut they had still been mortared tightly together in massive blocks, each Knox's height or taller, and none had corners or lips protruding more than a finger's width. If he'd had bird talons for feet instead of regular toes wedged inside enormous boots, he probably could have scaled the thing in no time. As it was, Knox couldn't even pull himself up off the ground.

Hoping that perhaps the wall was only loosely joined to the manor, Knox followed it around until it reached the cliff. That was a disappointment as well, though — the first few blocks were carved out of the mountainside itself, so the wall blended seamlessly into that edifice. He could only assume that the other side was much the same. And the manor had no back or sides, so this was the only way in or out.

He would have to wait until Wednesday. Then he'd see if he couldn't sneak past Miche and Gerta and the others and convince this man Bartosz to bring him down the mountain.

On Wednesday morning, Knox approached Gerta. "I have my list here for Bartosz," he started, holding up a folded paper, "but there are a few things I need to explain myself."

Gerta frowned, but he'd come to realize this was simply her default expression. "Very well," she said after a moment. "When he arrives, you may speak with him."

Yes! But Knox did his best to show restraint. "Thanks. That'd be perfect."

He wished he'd been able to produce some gold coins with which to bribe the man, but his cap was still unwilling to oblige. Probably because they had not had rare beef since that first day, and even if he were able to distract Rolf and Liesel long enough to dip his cap in chicken blood or fish blood, it would not be quite the same. Knox was starting to feel the effects of going too long without renewing that grisly coloration, which was another reason he'd need help to escape.

When Danika came to tell him the old man was here with his deliveries, Knox leapt to his feet and followed her to the front door, reaching it just as Miche came through carrying two large burlap sacks. "He is outside, go now if you wish to give him your list," the dogsbody explained. Knox did so at once — and stopped just past the front steps, confused, because though the front gates were not quite closed anymore, he saw no one around.

Then a flicker of movement made him glance again. Something had moved just beyond the gate.

Stomping quickly forward, shivering as he went, Knox soon saw that the gates were open wide enough for a large man to squeeze through—or a man carrying several sacks. And beyond it stood an old man, heavily bundled in thick furs.

And holding the reins to a short, shaggy donkey.

"Ah!" the man said when he saw Knox. "You are the painter, yes? Miche said. You have list?" His accent was very thick and his voice very raspy, but Knox still understood him well enough.

"Aye," he replied. "I'm Knox. I do have me list here. But I've got some tricky bits about it. Can ye no' come in out of the cold and we'll talk abut them?" He couldn't very well bribe the man out here in the open!

But the old man—clearly Bartosz—shook his head. "No, no, Herr vom Berge does not allow anyone else through the gates," he said quickly, backing up a pace for good measure. "I wait here. You give me list, I go get for you."

The man was clearly terrified, and for an instant Knox wondered if he knew Rübezahl's true nature, but perhaps it was just the fear of a rich and stern patron. Regardless, he obviously wasn't going to be bribing Bartosz into helping. There also wasn't exactly any place to hide on the donkey.

For a second, standing there at the open gate, Knox considered just making a break for it. He could run quickly, even in his present state. If he just charged down the road, could he get far enough to win free before Rübezahl realized he'd gone and came after him?

Except that it had taken hours to get up here, and that had been by car. Nor could he remember if there had been only one road, or how clearly marked it had been. Obviously, Miche knew the way, just as Bartosz and his donkey did. But on his own, without any help or guidance? Knox would be lost within the hour. Stranded high on a mountain, with nothing to eat and no shelter, nowhere to escape the cold. He'd freeze to death. That wasn't the answer.

Accepting defeat for the moment, Knox handed Bartosz his list. "These are what I need," he said. "Thank you."

As he turned away, he caught a glimpse of a dark shape in one of the turreted upper windows. Herr vom Berge, also known as Rübezahl. Keeping an eye on him.

Knox grimaced but returned to the house. What else could he do for now?

He wasn't giving up, though. There had to be a way out of here, and he'd figure it out. Somehow.

CHAPTER FOURTEEN

FOR TWO FULL DAYS, KNOX SCOURED THE HOUSE AND THE GROUNDS, seeking a way out.

He found nothing.

The house's water came from an artesian well, set in its own small alcove at the back of the kitchen. The little fountain bubbled up there, ice-cold and crystal-clear, and fed from that point into copper pipes for the plumbing, while Rolf and Liesel scooped out buckets for use in the daily dishes, and to drink besides. But the water's exit point was narrow, no larger than Knox's fist, and it burst upward with enough force that nothing could be pushed back down even if there was enough room. No escape there.

The manor was big and drafty, so there were fireplaces here and there, but in each case the chimney narrowed to a chute no wider than a small cat. And even if Knox were somehow able to work his way up one, it would come out on top of the mountain, leaving him stranded up there. That would be even worse than getting stuck after making it over the walls.

If there was a river, he might have considered trying to fashion a boat or at least a raft. Growing up on the loch, Knox could handle himself on the water. He'd been a solid swimmer as a youth, too, but that wasn't possible anymore with the iron boots.

Could he fashion some sort of parachute or glider to take him from up here down the mountain to a town or road, even with the weight of the boots? Perhaps, but without knowing the local geography he could smack into the side of the mountain, get tangled up in trees, or drift out to sea. No thanks.

A sled, then, to glide down the road? Again, he didn't know the route—one hairpin turn and he'd be done for.

He kept coming back to the idea of just making a break for it, shoving past Bartosz the next time the old man showed with supplies and running flat out for as long as he could, as far as he could. But that always led to images of Rübezahl stalking after him, grown to a giant with arms long as the twilight and claws the size of scythes, and dragging him back kicking and screaming to be locked inside an iron cage and fed only when he painted. At least for now he still had the freedom of the house.

Still, not finding a way out had his spirits at low ebb, and Knox stumbled about, going from bed to breakfast to roaming and eventually back to bed again, sometimes with another meal in between.

He was staring aimlessly at one of the manor's massive, ornately carved fireplaces when Gerta found him.

"You must stop this," she warned, planting herself in front of him so he had no choice but to see her stern expression. "It does you no good, and you waste away because of it."

"He's a monster," Knox replied. He was too far gone now to care about being circumspect, even if it meant his life.

He was surprised, though, when the housekeeper nodded. "Yes, he can be," she agreed, her voice pitched low but clear. "When he is unhappy. Thus, it is best to keep him happy."

"I cannae." Knox tried to make her understand. "He killed me friends to get me here. How kin I work for someone like tha'?"

"How can you not?" she countered. "You already know what he is capable of. Do you wish to provoke him further?" She patted his shoulder, the motion awkward. She was not often given to such gestures. "It is not so bad a life here, is it? You are comfortable? And you have found some kinship among us? Plus, you have your art to keep you busy. Perhaps, when it is done, he will let you leave. Even if only for a little while. But if you anger him…" She frowned. "I do not wish to think what he might do."

Knox had a sudden image of Rübezahl breaking his legs so that he had to drag himself forward with his arms to paint. Or, even worse, harming Danika or Miche or one of the others as a way of punishing him for his rebellion. He shuddered. "Aye, ye may be right. Perhaps it be safest to capitulate."

She nodded, but did him the kindness of not beaming. They both knew it was not a win so much as a sensible choice. "Good. I will see you at dinner, then, yes? In the kitchens, as usual?"

He nodded. And, when the evening meal rolled around, he was there. Being around her and the others did help, somewhat.

The next day, he returned to his sketches. And, when Bartosz arrived the following Wednesday with paints and brushes, Knox got to work in earnest.

Gerta was right, the art did help. It kept him busy but also occupied his thoughts, figuring out which shades to mix and where to apply shadows and how to simulate motion and so on. At the end of each day, he was exhausted, too tired to be upset about his predicament.

Not that he forgot about it. But he did his best to make peace with the situation. For now.

After a few weeks, Knox noticed something. "It's Monday, and we had rare roast beef," he commented to Rolf after dinner that night. "We had that two weeks ago, too. And that first time, two weeks before that."

The cook nodded quickly, but looked away as he said, "Yes, master's orders. Rare beef every second Monday. Is special for you. You like, yes?"

"Yes. Thank you." But Knox understood the real reasoning behind the menu choice, even if Rolf didn't. He'd been weak as a kitten when he woke this morning, his cap nearly dry. Now, having dunked it in the runoff from the meat over by the sink while washing up, he was at least healthy again. And it looked as if that would keep him going, though with diminishing strength, for another two weeks— just in time for the same meal to be served again. Rübezahl was rationing the myoglobin—Knox had looked it up after the encounter in the creature's study— giving him just enough to stay alive but not enough to ever be even close to full strength, which reduced the chance of him escaping. It was carefully calculated indeed. And Knox couldn't refuse it, since to do so would leave him ill, incapacitated, and eventually dead.

Several more weeks passed, and one day Knox turned from studying the rough outlines he'd painted to find Rübezahl himself standing just inside the doorway, leaning on his ever-present cane.

"I am liking this very much, Mister Adair," the master of the house told him. "Very much indeed. Keep up the excellent work." He turned and left without another word, the cane clicking on the floor between his footsteps, and Knox knew that was another message: I can be stealthy when I wish, so you will only hear me coming if that is my intent.

Furious at being caught out like that—and at appreciating the compliment, even from one such as that—Knox slammed his fist into a paint can he'd perched on the ladder beside him. "Damn it all!" The dented can toppled, deluging him with its contents before he managed to catch it and set it on the floor. At least he'd thought to put down drop cloths, or he'd be trying to scrape it up off the parquet tiles!

As he straightened, though, Knox felt an oddly familiar tingling. It started at his brow but swept down through his whole body, leaving him feeling—strong. Energized. More so than he had since... since he'd left home. It felt as if he'd just dipped his cap, but not in fish blood or even cow's blood. No, this felt nearly as good as if he'd used the blood of a human.

But how?

Staring at the can, and at his own hands, Knox saw them all awash in red, vivid as a flame. It was definitely paint, though. He could tell by the sharp, acrid smell of it, and the feel on his skin. Standard bright red oil paint. Tugging off his cap, he saw that it was indeed saturated with the stuff.

And that's when Knox remembered something he'd read while researching paint colors:

Oil paint never dried.

Not really, anyway. Acrylics and watercolors dried when the water evaporated, leaving the pigment behind. Oil paints oxidized instead, hardening but never actually drying out. Which was why you could still manipulate oil paint, even years later.

And red paint was made with iron oxide. Iron and oxygen, two of the key ingredients found in blood.

It wasn't the same, of course. And Knox suspected that, if he were to go toe to toe with one of his kin like Logan or Brodie, he'd still come up short. But compared to how he usually felt, this was amazing. He was stronger than right after either of his two previous solutions, and his cap could conceivably stay saturated from a single coat for months or even years.

This was a gamechanger—and he owed it, in a way, to Rübezahl's surprise visit. Far from intimidating him, the mountain spirit had accidentally offered him at least part of a way out.

Knox just had to figure out how to use it.

Chapter Fifteen

KNOX STARED AT THE SCREEN, UTTERLY TRANSFIXED, AS A SLIM, DARK-haired man leapt up, somehow bounced up and over a wall, dove through a narrow window, used a rope to run sideways along a wall, and jumped from rooftop to rooftop. How the actual hell? Was he another supernatural? Or was it just movie magic?

Over the past year, Knox had at least taken advantage of his enforced employment to learn about something he'd never known before and now had ready access to—technology. At least of the entertainment variety. The television in his room got all sorts of channels, and he spent at least an hour a day watching something on it, trying to familiarize himself more with the world of mortals. He'd quickly learned that Kinglassie had been very small and more than a little backward, with its stores still using mechanical cash registers and the houses still having landlines. Through TV shows and movies, he found out about cell phones and thumb drives and much more.

His favorite, though, were the movies. When watching one, Knox could forget where he was and why, at least for the duration. This one had only come to television recently, and it appeared to be some sort of futuristic action film. But the stunts! They were amazing!

After watching the whole movie, Knox turned to the computer. He'd learned how to use that properly as well, and it only took him a few seconds to turn up an astonishing truth—all the stunts had been real! Apparently the two lead actors practiced a new kind of urban sport called parkour, which was the art of using an urban landscape as a sort of obstacle course. It was absolutely fascinating.

And Knox saw the potential use for such a skill immediately.

Though it had taken far longer than he might have liked in better circumstances, he'd eventually finished sketching out all of the basic lines for his mural. The great hall was enormous, though, with its ceiling easily forty feet off the ground, so he'd been forced to assemble scaffolding to reach the upper walls.

The morning after watching that film, Knox considered those metal and plywood platforms with a new eye. He had the boots to deal with, of course, but thanks to his beloved oil paint he was stronger and faster than any human, and a good deal more durable. Now, eyeing the nearest scaffold, he took a deep breath, and another.

Then he took a running leap and grabbed hold of a crossbar at least two meters off the ground.

Hauling himself up, he shoved his legs forward and slid onto the platform there, letting go of the bars as he passed beneath them. He bounded to his feet and then rolled forward, diving over the bars to that side—

—and landing flat on his back on the platform below, knocking the wind out of him.

Still, he found himself grinning as he lay there, gasping for breath. That was more fun than he'd had in a long time! And not a bad attempt for his first try.

It might take him a while to get good at it, but he had nothing but time. And being able to climb and leap like that, well, what better way to scale a large stone wall?

* * *

Another year passed. Knox had roughed in the entire mural and was now going back and applying additional layers of color and shading and detail. He'd gotten good enough at parkour that he could bounce all over the scaffolding and around the room without pause. He was careful to only do that when no one else was around, though. Best to keep his new talents—and his restored strength—to himself.

He was fairly certain he could get over the wall now. The problem was, what to do then? He'd still be stuck at the top of the mountain, with no way down and no idea where to go. And no money.

"I just need a few coins, just a few," he muttered, spinning his cap on one finger before upending it and groping around inside. His fingers encountered nothing but heavy wool, however. The oil paint might keep him strong and healthy, but it still wouldn't yield any gold.

Then again, maybe gold wasn't what he needed. That was old-world thinking, his family's way of thinking. But who really used gold and silver anymore? What if he tried for something else? Something less cumbersome?

Knox had never really known how the cap's magic worked. It just did. You dipped your cap in blood, reached into it, and pulled out gold coins. But maybe that was just because the Red Caps expected that kind of currency?

Now, cap clutched between his fingers, he closed his eyes and concentrated. Not on gold, though. Not even on pennies and shillings. No, this time he thought about something other than the cold, hard feel of metal.

Instead, he imagined the crinkling of bills, the worn texture of old, well-used bank notes.

Paper money. A modern thing his family scorned, but far more common and more useful in today's world.

Knox tried to imagine one in his hand. The way it felt against his skin, the way he could trace the outline of it, the way the corners bent at his touch.

And then he could feel it for real. Removing his hand slowly, like he was afraid to wake a butterfly sleeping there, Knox unbent his fingers—

—and stared at the five-pound note crumpled there against his palm.

He'd done it!

It took a bit more practice to draw forth euros instead, since he'd never handled one himself, but eventually Knox had the knack of it down. Now he had money, health, strength, and climbing.

He just needed a way down off the mountain.

Bartosz was still bringing supplies, but the old man was visibly growing too frail to keep making the long journey up and back. One Wednesday, he appeared with another man at his side. This one was significantly younger, though still at least forty, and though bigger and thicker he didn't have the same seasoned toughness. They shared enough features, though, that Knox wasn't surprised when the old man introduced the newcomer as "my son, Szymon."

The son nodded to Miche and Knox and Gerta and Rolf, the four who typically carted in the supplies—Knox had taken to helping with this as an excuse to get outside, even if only for a few minutes. "My father is getting too old for this trek," Szymon said in Polish, which Knox had learned enough to understand by now. "I will take over the deliveries." He did not sound particularly thrilled with the idea, but Knox knew Rübezahl—he only ever thought of his employer as such, though he had never spoken that name aloud since that first time—paid very, very well. Well enough to make it worth the man's while to continue providing that service.

For the next two weeks, Szymon arrived with Bartosz, helping his father unload the donkey. The week after that, Szymon came alone.

If Knox had hoped the son would be any easier to bribe than the father, he was soon disappointed. Though Szymon did not seem as frightened of Rübezahl as Bartosz had been, still he wasn't about to jeopardize his very lucrative job. Besides which, even if he'd wanted to help Knox, how could he? There was still just the one donkey, though this too was a newer, younger beast than the original.

But two months after Szymon took over, Knox heard a strange sound out on the mountain beyond the wall. He recognized the noise at once, from all the shows and movies he'd watched, but he'd never heard it out here, not since he'd first arrived.

It was the sound of a car approaching.

Rushing out front, he waited, almost twitching with excitement, as a bright red SUV appeared around the bend and drove right up to the gate, stopping just shy of hitting it. A man climbed out, and at first Knox thought it was Szymon, but as he closed the distance it became evident this man was much younger, probably around Knox's age. His hair was cut short, and he had a neat beard to match, but otherwise he looked too much like Szymon to be anyone but his son.

"Hey, I'm Eddie," the newcomer announced, offering a hand to each of the waiting staff in turn. "Szymon's son. He's not feeling great, so I'm taking over with the deliveries."

"Nice SUV," Knox told him, and Eddie grinned.

"It is, right? My dad was all 'you must take the donkey, it is tradition,' but I told him, I said, 'what is this, the Middle Ages?' No way I'm dragging a donkey all the way up here when I can ride in style!"

Knox nodded, but he only had eyes for the brightly colored vehicle as they unloaded it and Eddie helped stack the groceries by the gate so the others could carry them in. It did look comfortable, but more importantly, it had a lot of space tucked away in back. Space for groceries—or for one Red Cap looking to get away quickly.

The final piece of his plan had just arrived.

CHAPTER SIXTEEN

THREE MONTHS LATER, KNOX FINISHED THE MURAL. GERTA, MICHE, AND even Hans helped him take down the scaffolding, disassembling each tower of platforms and pipes and stacking them neatly off to one side. When all of that was cleared away, they all stood in the center of the room, staring at the fully revealed artwork wrapping around the enormous room.

"It's amazing!" Danika gushed, looking wide-eyed this way and that as if desperate to take it all in at once. "I feel like I'm standing in the middle of the forest!"

"Indeed, but no forest I've ever seen," Miche corrected, his voice hushed. The older man—his hair had mostly turned gray over the nearly three years Knox had known him—had his own cap clutched in his hands, which trembled slightly now, but the smile he gave Knox was beatific. "You've done well, lad. It's a marvel, truly."

"I would have to agree." The announcement, quiet though it was, startled all of them, the pack of servants scattering like pigeons spying a hungry cat. Only Knox forced himself to stand still as Herr vom Berge/Lord John/Rübezahl stalked into the room to join him, cane tapping at his side. "It is a true masterpiece, Mister Adair," the master of the house told him. "I am both impressed and gratified. Well done."

"Thanks." Looking up at it all, the years of toil and creation, Knox had to admit that he was proud of what he'd done here. It really did feel like being in the forest at twilight in autumn, as the leaves were starting to change color almost as if to match the shades the sun cast across the sky. But then, as Miche said, you started to realize this was no normal forest. Small creatures peered out from behind leaves and atop branches, or blended into tree boughs and hanging vines. They were small, subtle, but once you noticed them you couldn't help looking for more — and finding them, often in the oddest places.

Yes, he was very happy with this, the greatest artwork he'd ever produced.

Which was why he turned to his host now. "Since ye're so keen on it, I'd say the job's done, yeah? Time for me to move on, and then some."

He hadn't expected Rübezahl to agree too easily. But he was still surprised when the mountain spirit masquerading as a man laughed. Nor was it entirely a happy sound, though certainly there were notes of mirth mixed in among it.

"Oh, Mister Adair, I thought you understood the full scope of your task," the master of the house said once he'd recovered from his bout of amusement. "This is the largest room, certainly, but not the only one. There are many rooms to Berghaus, after all, and I did tell you this was but the first." He tapped a forefinger against his lip. "I think perhaps the dining room next, hm? But first I will enjoy this transformative piece a while longer." That was clearly a dismissal and Knox took it, hurrying away before his blood boiled over and made him do something stupid.

It wasn't like he hadn't anticipated something like this. After all, what had the man told him, all those years ago? "The only one to have a mural painted by a Red Cap." The art would lose some of its uniqueness if Knox was out in the world, painting for others, and Rübezahl was far too much the consummate collector to not take that as a personal affront.

It had taken almost three years to paint the great room. Even if the other rooms were not quite so grand, Knox could still be looking at a year or two apiece on them. And with dozens of other rooms, maybe more... he could be here for decades.

Assuming Rübezahl ever intended to let him leave at all.

But that was fine. Knox was not unprepared. He'd been careful to budget his time. Today was Tuesday. Eddie would be here with supplies in the morning. And they'd had beef the Monday before last, meaning the master would expect Knox's cap to be more than half dry by now, leaving him weak as a kitten.

Everything was ready. He'd deliberately waited, giving the man a chance to let him go.

Now Knox would just have to do things the hard way.

The next morning, he rose early and was waiting when the SUV pulled up to the gates, as usual. By now Eddie had grown used to the routine. He didn't try engaging Gerta in conversation, and neither Miche nor Rolf were inclined to chat with the relative newcomer. Knox tended to carry things in quickly as well, initially to avoid staying by the vehicle so long he did something stupid and then so he wouldn't draw attention to his interest. Today was no different—until they'd carried the last of the parcels inside. Then Knox straightened and clapped Miche on the shoulder.

"Gonna stretch me legs a little," he told the old dogsbody. "Ye good?"

"No worries," the older man confirmed, lugging the last bag. "Take your time." He walked away without a second glance.

Knox felt torn at that. Despite Rübezahl's bloodthirsty and possessive ways, there had been good things about being here at Berghaus. And one of those—one of the big ones—had been Miche and Gerta and the others. Their company had helped get him through his confinement. He was going to miss them all.

Assuming he even survived this.

He turned away—and almost bumped into Gerta. The housekeeper was watching him, arms folded over her chest, braids swaying in the wind. "What are you about?" she asked softly.

"Just getting some air," he answered, trying for nonchalance. But she shook her head.

"No. Just now—that was a good-bye." Her eyes narrowed. "You are leaving." He didn't answer, but he didn't have to. They both knew the truth already.

Then, suddenly, she lunged forward and wrapped him in a quick, fierce hug. "Go," she whispered in his ear. "Be free. Live well. And know you will be missed."

Though surprised, Knox reacted quickly enough to hug her back. "Thank ye. I'll miss all o' ye, as well." He swallowed past the lump in his throat, feeling the need to explain more, but Gerta had already disengaged and called out to Eddie, "I have just remembered another thing I must have. Wait here."

She was giving him an opening, Knox knew. One he couldn't count on ever having again. He wasn't about to waste it.

Glancing up at the turret and seeing its windows empty, he hurried along the wall until he'd reached the corner where it met the house and the mountain. Then, calling upon the skills he'd perfected on the scaffolding, Knox threw himself up into the air. He twisted mid-leap, kicking out with one foot and pushing off from the cliff face, propelling himself higher. Another kick, this time on the wall itself, and then a third against the house—and his hands grasped a wide, rough-hewn stone lip.

He'd reached the top of the wall.

Not allowing himself to pause and lose precious momentum, Knox swung himself over that broad expanse and dropped straight down, bending his knees and tucking into a ball at the last minute. He hit the ground hard but rolled with the impact, springing to his feet and then sprinting for the SUV. He was out, but not away yet!

Eddie hadn't locked the vehicle—no need when there was no one else around and he stood only a few feet away—and Knox was able to open the trunk and duck inside, pulling it shut again behind him. There was a screen back here, usually pulled forward to shield the produce from the sun, and he slid under that now, where no one would be able to see him from inside the car or out.

Then he waited.

A moment later, he heard voices. Then the car door opening. It closed, and the engine revved. The SUV lurched into motion, reversing and turning until it faced back down the mountain.

And then they were off.

Knox couldn't see anything but the car's otherwise empty trunk. He couldn't hear anything beyond the rush of the wind, the roar of the engine, the thrum of the tires—and then the loud rock music Eddie turned on and began singing along to. Badly.

Despite being wound tight as a spool of thread, Knox closed his eyes and eventually fell into an uneasy sleep. He didn't wake until the car shuddered to a halt. It was dark beyond his hiding place. He heard a *click*, then a nearby motor, and the SUV jolted forward again, but only for a minute before it stopped. This time Eddie shut the engine off and climbed out, locking the doors with a *click* before Knox heard the motor again.

He was alone in the dark.

Carefully, quietly, he rolled out from under the screen and tried the trunk. It was locked. Wonderful. It took a minute or two before he could work his way over the back seat and tug at the door handle there. Also locked, but he found the manual release, flipped it, and popped the door open. There wasn't any noise beyond, so Knox slipped out of the car, shutting the door carefully behind him.

He was in a garage, he could tell that much. A row of small windows up high behind the car let in a little light from outside, and a thin line of brighter light ahead and to one side along the ground suggested a home beyond. Knox turned away from that, edging carefully toward the outside instead. He found the garage door and felt his way along it until his fingers brushed a lip he recognized as a doorframe. There was a knob at the usual height and he turned that, easing the door open and letting in a blast of cool, fresh air. Not as cold as at Berghaus, however. They weren't in the mountains here.

With only a second's hesitation, Knox slipped out of the garage and into the cold night. Now he really was free. He could hardly believe it.

But he also knew he couldn't relax yet. Rübezahl had a long reach and a vengeful nature. The sooner Knox was far away from here, the better.

Chapter Seventeen

Kinglassie looked much the same, Knox thought as he walked along Main Street. There was the grocer's, where he'd buy fruit and veg and bread to supplement the leftover cuts of fish Linda let him have for free. Past that was the druggist's. Across the way was the Oxfam, and beyond that the little corner store.

And there was the shop with its sign saying "Fish" above the door.

That door had been repainted a cheery blue at some point, he noticed, but his eyes went to the bottom and he couldn't help wondering if that had been to cover up the blood. Had Linda's death permanently stained the shop she'd created? Or had a new owner simply wished to distinguish themselves from their ill-fated predecessor?

He didn't go in. But, as he turned away, he noticed something stuck in the front window, a small poster now yellowed with age. "Have you seen this man?" bold letters asked across the top, above a rough sketch of a youngish man with long hair beneath a broad, slouching cap. "Wanted in connection with several suspicious deaths. If seen, notify the local constabulary at once" was in slightly smaller print below that.

Knox tugged the hood of his jacket lower, making sure his face was well within shadow and his hair tucked away behind his neck, and hurried away.

He wasn't sure why he'd come back, really. He'd known there'd be nothing for him here. Not to mention, anyone who watched crime shows and mysteries knew that one of the golden rules was, "Never return to the scene of the crime." But somehow, he couldn't resist. This had been home, in many ways far more than Castle Lachlan ever had. And he thought he owed it to the Travers to stop by one last time.

Besides, once he'd escaped the mountains, he hadn't anywhere else to go.

It had taken long enough to get here. First, he'd trekked north, all the way through Poland to the port of Szczecin at the very southern edge of the Baltic Sea. Without ID or any money beyond that handful of euros, he'd resigned himself to walking the whole way, though he'd managed to hitch a ride once or twice and had hopped a railcar once as well. He'd also had a brief stop in a town not far outside Berlin, and had remained there for almost two weeks before a chance encounter had nearly proven fatal. After that, Knox knew he had to get out of the country, and fast. Upon reaching the open water, he'd been strangely comforted — that was more like the loch back home, though far larger — and had sought out the fishing boats plying their trade along the coast, hoping for something similar to the work he'd had with Linda.

Most of the ship captains wouldn't even talk to him once they found he didn't speak more than a few words in Polish. But one, upon hearing his accent, had taken pity on him. "A fellow Brit, eh?" the man had said around the short, stubby cigar he chewed upon. "Lemme guess, victim a' some misadventure, no money and no ID and desperate to get home?"

"Something like that," Knox had agreed. "Kin ye help me? I'll work for me passage, o' course. I'm good at fish."

The captain had eyed him up and down. "Aye," he'd said finally. "Lucky for ye, I'm shorthanded at the moment. We work both the Baltic and the North Seas, either side o' Denmark, and once or twice a year I put in at Aberdeen. I'll not be hurrying on yer account, though, so's ya know. But do the work and I'll get ye there."

"Fair enough," Knox had replied, offering his hand. That was how he'd wound up serving under Captain Alistair McNee on the *Clever Carp* for six months. But eventually they had indeed crossed the North Sea and docked at Aberdeen, where McNee had handed him a wad of cash.

"Yer a good lad," the fishing boat captain had told him. "Good luck to ya."

Knox had used some of that money to take the train from Aberdeen to Perth and had walked to Kinglassie from there. The question, of course, was what to do next. He couldn't linger very long here, and didn't want to, not without the Travers and even Linda. But wherever he went after this, he'd felt it was important to at least say good-bye.

With that in mind, he made his way down Main Street to a familiar corner, his feet still knowing the way. Taking the turn, he glanced up — and froze.

Because all that was left of the Travers' beloved café was a blackened ruin.

A monstrous fire had clearly engulfed the place at some point, hot enough to cave in the walls and bring the roof crashing in. The windows had all shattered, and the walls were dark with soot and grime, what bits of them were still standing. Any trace of his dragon mural was long since gone, as were all the cheery little notes that the Travers had used to make the place so warm and welcoming.

Their business was as dead as they were.

Even so, Knox found himself approaching it, crossing the street and stepping onto the familiar brick patio where he'd first met Edin and then Rory. He wandered over to the café in a daze, entering it through the empty doorframe which yawed dangerously to one side. The counter was gone as well, vanished beneath brick and mortar and wood and shingle from the fallen roof, and glass and splinters crackled beneath his feet. To the left had been the small dining room, and peering into the shadows Knox was shocked to see that a single table and chair remained in the exact center of that rubble-strewn space.

A tall, lean man sat there, ramrod straight, hands toying with the silver head of his ebon cane.

"You have taken your time, Mister Adair," that familiar chilly voice drifted across to him. "I have been waiting here for some time now." Rübezahl rose to his feet. Knox screamed at himself to run but couldn't move, staring as his former employer approached. "I was not completely sure you would even return here. It was foolishly sentimental of you to do so."

"Ye did this," Knox accused, finding his voice again at least. "Ye burned it all down."

The mountain spirit did not bother to deny it. "Of course. As I told you, I wished to be the only one with a mural by a Red Cap." His grin was a faint hint of lighter shapes in the shadows. "Besides, they hardly needed it any longer, hm?"

"Because ye killed them." Anger freed his limbs, but instead of fleeing Knox stomped forward to meet the man, glaring up at him. "Ye killed them!"

Rübezahl was unfazed by his tone, or his words. "One could argue that *you* killed them, by refusing my initial offer," he stated, but deep inside Knox knew that wasn't true. To have Knox's only work, the spirit would have had to kill them and destroy this place, regardless. Though that still laid the ultimate blame for those deaths squarely at Knox's ironshod feet.

"Now," Rübezahl continued. "Are you prepared to return and continue your work for me?" His eyes gleamed blue and cold. "Or shall this be the end of our relationship?"

Knox could guess what that meant. An artist's work was almost always worth more after their death, after all. Even so, standing here of all places, there was no way he could even pretend to agree. "I'll never work for ye again," he said instead, clenching his fists. "Just go back and leave me alone."

The shadows seemed thicker now, colder, and the man before him even taller. "That I cannot do," he intoned. "For I will not have you sharing your art with others. It is mine, and mine alone."

The shift in air warned Knox just in time, and he spun, cartwheeling to the side as Rübezahl's oversized, clawed hand lashed out right where his chest had been. One boot tip clipped a shattered table that had somehow survived the conflagration, iron striking sparks against the bent metal leg, and the shards of wood still connected to that caught fire, casting a sudden, warm glow around the room.

Knox's attacker shrank back from it.

Even as his mind grasped that fact, Knox crouched. He yanked the makeshift torch free and up before him, brandishing it in Rübezahl's face. Of course. The mountain spirit was one with earth and stone—and cold. Fire was anathema to him. Hence the constant chill at Berghaus, and even in his plane and train and car.

"That little fire will not burn forever," Herr vom Berge warned, looming over him but temporarily held at bay. "And I am patient. I will have you, little Red Cap, or no one will."

"Ye'll have to wait a long time, then," Knox snapped, backing away toward the door. "An' I'll be watching for ye."

Then he'd darted through, out into the open air. Tossing the torch back into the café behind him, he turned and ran for his life.

Chapter Eighteen

The man glared at Knox over his clipboard. "Little fella, eh? Can ya pull yer weight?"

In answer, Knox turned to a nearby stack of full barrels, their sides slick from ocean spray and fish guts, and hoisted one up onto his shoulder. "Try me."

"Fair enough. ID?"

Knox set the barrel down — carefully, the last thing he needed was to break it and cost the fishing boat money! — before pulling out his wallet and extracting a card from it. He'd spent all the rest of his cash buying that, and hoped it would pass muster, but the man barely glanced at it before handing it back and writing Knox's name on his list. "Job pays twenty an hour," he explained. "Four weeks at sea, working eight-hour shifts six days a week, you get paid when we dock in New York. Meals're covered, and yer berth. Gloves and rainslickers we've got, rest of yer clothes are on you. Sign here." And he handed the clipboard over.

Glancing at it quickly, Knox signed and returned it. "When do we leave?"

"Four tomorrow morning," was the reply, and Knox nodded. He'd kept back just enough cash to buy a few more pairs of clothes, and obviously he had the boot part covered, so he figured he'd pick up those last few items, then either find a cheap bed for the night or just crash out here on the docks so he could be on hand for launch.

And then a month at sea and he'd reach America. Well beyond Rübezahl's grasp, or so he hoped.

As he went about his business, Knox couldn't help thinking back on the other stop he'd made before coming here to Oban. It had been strange hiking openly through Queen Elizabeth Forest Park, looking much like any other young backpacker with his jeans, boots, and rucksack, but far stranger had been trekking down the loch until the familiar ruins had come into view. Castle Lachlan had looked exactly the same from there, just as rundown as ever and, at least to anyone watching, just as empty. But of course Knox knew better.

A part of him had wanted to approach the place, to pound on the gates and demand that Great-uncle Karson let him in. He'd wanted to show them all that he was still alive. Not only that, but doing well, healthy and whole without needing to murder animals or people. But he'd guessed what most of them would say, how they'd treat him.

There was only one person he'd wanted to see, really. He couldn't risk it, of course. But he'd still felt he should at least let her know he was okay.

So, Knox had taken out his sketchpad and drawn a quick image of two Red Caps sitting together at the top of the old tower, legs dangling over the side: him and Elidh, much as they'd been right before he left. But he updated his image to match how he looked now, with his new clothes and backpack and his hair neatly combed and brushed back.

Then he'd snuck around to the castle's far side. There was a spot there where they'd liked to go for a moment's peace and quiet and, conveniently, to gather wild garlic. None of the others knew about it, Knox didn't think, so he'd felt comfortable carefully folding the paper and tucking it beneath the crumbling lip of an empty window frame there. It would stay dry until Elidh found it. Even if someone else somehow spotted it first, there weren't any words, nothing to date it, so it easily could be from before he'd left. But he felt confident his sister would notice the differences and get the message.

There was little more he could do without risking a fight and various other troubles, so he'd left it at that, trekking away from the place before any of his kin could see him.

He knew he wouldn't ever return.

———◗▬▬———

"Can you believe it?" Luis said, elbowing Knox where they stood at the trawler's prow, watching as it motored into the harbor. "New York City!"

Behind them, Timmy snorted, then stopped as someone cuffed him upside the head. Probably Manny. "Leave 'em alone," the other fisherman warned, just loud enough for Knox to hear. "Your first time seeing it, you wept like a baby."

"Did not!" Timmy insisted, but he didn't give them any more grief. And they'd already finished all their chores, so they were free to stand there gawking at the front rail if they wished.

Which Knox did. He thought he'd become inured to new sights from his travels, and from all the shows he'd watched. But seeing New York City in person? It turned out that was a whole other thing.

It was so big! So tall, at any rate. The buildings towered up, up, up into the sky, their spires scraping the clouds, and this while the boat still approached. He could only imagine what it was like looking up at them from the city streets. They all looked so grand, too, but so different, some of them sleek stone while others were sharp-edged glass and still others were heavily ornamented. It was fascinating.

"Right!" That was Palmer, the ship's first mate, and Knox and Luis turned reluctantly to give him their attention instead as the other fishermen also gathered round. "For the newcomers, here's the drill. We dock, unload, then head to the hotel. Once we're all checked in, I'll hand out your pay. Tomorrow, you'll get four hours of shopping and sightseeing, supervised by me, the captain, or one of the shipping company reps. Day after, same thing. Breakfasts and dinners are covered at the hotel, same as the rooms. Three days from now, we head back out. If you choose not to sign up for the return trip, you'll have ten days to find another gig or they'll deport you back to wherever you call home. Got it?"

Everyone nodded, though Knox frowned, as did Luis beside him. "I can't go back, man," Luis whispered to him. "I got bad debts, you know? I signed on for a clean start here."

Knox felt the same way. Fortunately, Manny had lingered near them. "Don't worry about it," the more experienced sailor told them, his voice low. "You'll be fine, you'll see." He was the one who'd taken them under his wing when they'd set out from Oban, teaching them the trick of working a big commercial trawler, helping them settle in, so Knox figured he'd trust the man for now. Worse came to worst, he could probably break himself out, and maybe Luis along with him.

The unloading took a few hours, and they were all exhausted and filthy by the time they headed to the hotel, which proved to be a big, plain, square building. The windows all had bars on them and the stairwells and elevators required keys to open and operate, but the rooms were clean enough, with two beds and a bathroom for each.

Knox was put in with Gus, which was fine by him, as they got along well. Luis had been paired with Manny.

Knox had just showered and switched to clean clothes when Palmer knocked on the door.

"Sign here," he said to each of them, handing over thick envelopes of cash once they had. "Food's on the way, should be here in a few, we've got a room at the end of the hall where we can eat. Come on over when you're ready."

Once Palmer had left, Knox glanced in his envelope, flicking through the thick stack of American dollar bills there, mostly hundreds but a few fifties and some twenties. Then he stuck the envelope in his back pocket and headed down the hall to see what New York food was like.

Later, as they were finishing their pizza — which Knox had enjoyed a great deal, all gooey and greasy — Manny nudged him. "Bunch of us're hitting the town after lights-out," he whispered. "You in?" Knox nodded. "Good deal. Just stick with Gus, he knows the way."

Two hours later, Palmer tapped on their door. "Lights out," the first mate called. But a few minutes later, Gus was up and moving. "Let's go." Knox followed him out into the hall and down to one of the stairwells, where Manny, Luis, and several others waited. Once they'd all gathered, Manny pulled out a key and unlocked the heavy metal door, ushering them all in. They took the concrete steps down to the ground floor, where he used the same key to open a door that led outside.

Once on the streets, Manny guided them up and over a few blocks, to a bar. Knox had been busy admiring the streets, the rows of houses and shops, the trees along the edges, all the people out and about. It was so busy here! Even at this late hour, the city bustled with life. He liked it.

And now that they were out of the hotel, he could easily disappear. His rucksack was still in the room but he had his pay and his ID, which was all he really needed. The rest he could replace.

The question was, should he stay here in New York? Or find someplace else to go? Well, he had a few days to make that decision. For tonight, Knox was determined to just relax and enjoy his first night in this famous city, out and about with his friends.

The next two days, they were allowed out to shop and explore the city, under strict supervision. Manny had explained that the first night, in the bar. "You gotta have a visa to be here if you aren't a citizen," he'd said. "Work or school, basically. We don't got either, 'cause we're only here between fishing trips. We're visiting, but for work. So they make sure we come in, do our job, and then ship out again. That's why all the locks and such. We're not supposed ta be out and about or we could sneak off." He'd winked. "Which is exactly what we're doing."

"I can't go back," Luis had told him then, and Manny had patted the other sailor's shoulder.

"No worries, man. We got you. Every trip, we got at least a few who wanna stay. You got anybody here?" Luis had shaken his head. "No sweat, a few of us know people. We'll give you some names, they can help you get settled, get a job, get ID, all that. What about you?" That last had been to Knox, and he'd frowned.

"I'm staying too," he'd said at last. "But maybe not here. Not sure yet. Might just explore the country a bit." He'd shrugged. He didn't really have a plan, other than not returning to the UK.

Now they were on their last night, so it was now or never. This time he'd brought his rucksack with him. They'd gone to a different bar each night, and now he bought a round of drinks for everyone. "It's been swell, lads," he said, hoisting his pint to them. "I'll miss ye, and I wish ye all well."

"Same to you, boyo," Gus replied, and the others echoed the sentiment. There were handshakes and backslaps all around, and Manny passed him and Luis slips of paper with some names and numbers on them. Then, not wanting to prolong things, Knox downed his beer and headed for the door.

Stepping outside, he took a deep breath. New York had a certain smell to it, he'd noticed. Car exhaust and metal and smoke from the subways and a mix of cooked food and, of course, the scent of millions of people all living in close proximity. It wasn't awful, but Knox felt oddly boxed in by the tall buildings and narrow streets. Besides which, this city was most people's first stop upon coming to the States. If Rübezahl ever did decide to come after him, it would the first place he'd look. No, better to move on.

So, shouldering his bag, Knox headed for a place he'd mentally marked during his "shopping" the day before: Port Authority. There were buses leaving all the time for cities all over the country.

Time to pick one and see where he wound up. Hopefully, it'd be somewhere interesting.

Chapter Nineteen

Knox stepped out of the bus station and took a big whiff of the air. *Hm.* Minneapolis had a crisp, clean smell to it, with lingering hints of winter and pine even now at the tail end of summer. He liked that.

It had taken him a full day to get here, switching from the first bus to a train and then back to a bus, but looking around, he thought it might have been worth it. Compared to New York, this city seemed almost small, and certainly closer to the ground, with far fewer skyscrapers. It also had wider streets and sidewalks, and a generally older, cozier feel. Plus, he'd passed over the river on the way in, the bus taking them across a wide, thick old stone bridge, and he liked that. It reminded him of the loch back home.

Not having any particular destination in mind, Knox picked a direction at random and started walking. It was well after dark and the sky loomed large overhead, the stars bright, which he also found comforting. In New York, he'd barely been able to see them for all the buildings crowding around.

"Hey. You." The voice interrupted his thoughts. Knox turned, surprised, to see someone stepping out of an alley he'd just passed. With few streetlights and most businesses already shut, he hadn't noticed the man.

Or... was he a man? He was tall, taller than most, and lean, almost sticklike. The way he moved was oddly disjointed, too, like his limbs lacked full mobility. As he approached Knox his features came into better view. They were boxy, rough, like someone's rude carving of a human.

Carved into wood, which the stranger's skin resembled.

"All right, mate, I've gotta ask," Knox said, hands going to his hips. "The hell're you? Sorry, don't mean ta be rude, only I've never seen a walking tree afore."

That stopped the stranger mid-stride, and he squinted down at Knox. "Ya can see me? Hell's bells, ya ain't human either, are ya? What'll ya be, then?"

"Red Cap," Knox answered, taking off his cap and twirling it around his finger for emphasis. "You?"

"Wulgaru. From Australia, eh?" The strange wood-man slumped a little. "Damn. Can't mug ya, then, can I?"

"Mug me? Is that what ye were doing?" Knox laughed. "Oy, mate, not sure how well that's working for ye. But here." He dug around in his cap and pulled out a crumpled bill, which he passed to the man. "There ya go."

"Hey, thanks!" The Wulgaru unfolded it, revealing a twenty. "Ya new here? Only, saw ya come from the bus station."

"Yep, just got in." Knox considered. This fellow hadn't seemed all that surprised to see a non-mortal, just disappointed. "Guessing I ain't the first critter ye've seen?"

That produced a laugh from the wood-man. "Ha, are ya kidding? City's lousy with us! Don't believe me, go see Mama Rheda. Down at Midtown Global Market." He rattled off an address, which Knox did his best to remember. "Anyway, cheers, mate. Seeya. And — welcome to the Twin Cities."

Knox watched the man amble off. So there were other supernaturals here, eh? That might be a very good thing for him. Needle in a haystack and all that. He'd see if he could find this "global market" and this Mama Rheda person, and see what's what.

Happy to have at least a temporary goal, Knox continued on down the road, whistling to himself as he went.

◆━━

"Nice work."

Knox glanced up to find a guy studying the drawing he'd just done. "Thanks." It was a park scene, and he'd drawn it right on the sidewalk, using large colored chalks. After seeing a few people doing something similar at a playground, he'd had the idea and was loving it so far. It was like a mural, but impermanent. Nothing for Rübezahl to be able to track down. The picture would fade with time and from people walking across it, but that was okay. Knox could always make a new one somewhere else.

"What're you, then?" the guy asked, stepping closer. He wasn't much taller than Knox but considerably beefier, his sleeveless black T showing off muscular arms covered in tattoos. He had buzzed-short blonde hair and almost golden tan skin. And, as he moved, something swished behind him. A tail.

Upon closer examination, the newcomer's skin also had an odd texture to it. Like scales? So, another supernatural, then.

"Red Cap," Knox replied, tapping the headwear in question. "From Scotland. Name's Knox, Knox Adair. You?" And he offered his hand. So far, most of the supernaturals he'd met here had been either casually welcoming or impersonally standoffish, and if this fellow was asking, he was at least the former.

"Kobold, originally out of Germany," came the reply, along with a firm handshake. "Name's Doug. Doug Ritter."

Knox cocked his head to the side. "Yer name's Dog?"

"Not dog, Doug." The guy's face wrinkled a bit, but he didn't look truly offended. "Anyway, I'm an artist, too. I paint."

"Yeah? Nice." Knox considered his picture, then the position of the sun. "Figuring to call it quits for the night, anyway. Wanna grab a beer, talk art?" He'd been here two weeks already and was just starting to scope out some of the better places to go. Having a local's opinion would go a long way.

Dog—that was now stuck in Knox's head—nodded. "Yeah, sure, why not?"

Together, the two of them walked away, leaving the park scene for anyone to admire or not, as they saw fit.

"Hey, Dougie Dog!" Knox called out, spotting his friend across the room.

As always, Doug grimaced at the nickname, but didn't do much more than shake his head. "What's up, Knox? How's the latest piece?"

"Good, man, good. How's the soul-sucking day job?" He'd learned, that first night, that while Doug was indeed a painter, he also had a legit job—as an auto refinisher. His work was amazing, too, but Knox kept telling the Kobold he should quit that and just concentrate on art full-time.

"Still paying the bills," Doug replied, raising his beer in salute. "Unlike you."

"Fair enough." Knox was able to scrounge enough bills from his cap to keep himself going, especially since he'd found a couple guys looking for a roommate to split an old converted loft. Mama Rheda had been a revelation that first day in the city, and had rented him a room without question, but his share of the loft was cheaper and gave him more space.

Plus, if Rübezahl ever did show up, the first place he'd check would be an entire apartment building filled with supernaturals. Better if Knox didn't make it that easy for him.

"So, what's shaking?" Knox asked now as he joined the Kobold. Over the past two months they'd started hanging out at least a few nights a week, occasionally with others Doug knew but mostly just the two of them. It really was good to know another artist. That was something Knox had never had before, not with Edin—not even with Elidh—and he loved getting to talk colors and designs with someone else. The fact that it was someone he didn't have to explain his true nature to—or hide it from—made it even better. He'd enjoyed his time in the kitchen at Berghaus—the only thing about that dreadful time he did like, other than the artwork itself—but he'd always felt he couldn't be his true self around them, not completely. Here, he could.

"Actually, I've got some news," Doug told him now. "My cousins are coming up to visit next month. Jeannie and Swift. You'll like them— they're artists, too. And Kobolds, obv."

"Nice." Knox accepted the beer the server had brought him, and took a sip. "Looking forward to it, mate. The more the merrier."

Yes, he decided once again. He'd definitely made the right choice coming here. The Twin Cities already felt like home. He couldn't wait to see what else this place had in store for him.

For More, Check out Yeti Left Home

"Rosenberg's tongue-in-cheek approach charms, creating an endearing, hirsute hero. Readers are sure to be entertained."
— Publishers Weekly

Small-Town Yeti, Big-City Problems

Peaceful, unassuming Wylie Kang—a Yeti with an appreciation for more *human* creature comforts—lives a quiet life in his self-built sanctuary on the outskirts of Embarrass, Minnesota. But when violent dreams disturb his peace, and a series of strange murders plague the area, a Hunter comes to town, nosing after Wylie's trail.

Fleeing pursuit, Wylie packs up his truck and heads for the Twin Cities, hoping to lose himself in the urban jungle, only to find a thriving supernatural community.

Just as he begins to settle in—with the help of some new-found friends—he discovers the bloodshed has followed… as has the Hunter.

Can Wylie catch the killer, before the Hunter catches him?

Available through all commercial booksellers

NEOPARADOXA
https://especbooks.square.site

About the Author

AARON ROSENBERG IS THE BEST-SELLING, AWARD-WINNING AUTHOR OF nearly 50 novels, including the DuckBob SF comedy series, the Relicant Chronicles epic fantasy series, the Areyat Islands fantasy pirate mystery series, the Yeti urban fantasy series, the *Dread Remora* space-opera series, and, with David Niall Wilson, the *O.C.L.T.* occult thriller series. His tie-in work contains novels for *Star Trek, Warhammer, World of WarCraft, Stargate: Atlantis, Shadowrun, Mutants & Masterminds,* and *Eureka and short stories for The X-Files, World of Darkness, Crusader Kings II, Deadlands, Master of Orion, and Europa Universalis IV.* He has written children's books (including the original series STEM Squad and Pete and Penny's Pizza Puzzles, the award-winning *Bandslam: The Junior Novel* and the #1 best-selling *42: The Jackie Robinson Story*), educational books on a variety of topics, and over 70 roleplaying games (including the original games *Asylum, Spookshow,* and *Chosen,* work for White Wolf, Wizards of the Coast, Fantasy Flight, Pinnacle, and many others, the Origins Award-winning *Gamemastering Secrets,* and the Gold ENnie-winning *Lure of the Lich Lord*). He is a founding member of Crazy 8 Press. Aaron lives in New York with his family.